Sisterhood of Swans

Sisterhood of Swans

SELMA CARVALHO

SPEAKING
TIGER

SPEAKING TIGER BOOKS LLP
125A, Ground Floor, Shahpur Jat,
New Delhi 110049

First published by Speaking Tiger Books in hardback 2021

ISBN: 978-93-5447-031-8
eISBN: 978-93-5447-036-3

10 9 8 7 6 5 4 3 2 1

Typeset in Minion Pro by SÜRYA, New Delhi
Printed at Chaman Enterprises, New Delhi

To Savio, Lauren & Misu

Contents

1

Funnelling into Darkness

The car swerves to the right of Hollyfield Road. The road is funnelling into darkness. Ines, my Mummy, is shaken up. I can tell. Beyond the immediate flared by headlights, I see nothing, I feel nothing. I am empty except for the thought that any minute now our car will hit a birch tree, its limbs will pierce my throat and the bark bruise-bleed my mouth. If there was a policeman treading the night, Francisco, my Daddy, might have slowed down. But up here, there is no one to stop the excesses of drink, the stale breath of used lives filling up the car.

When we reach home, Mummy takes me to bed, the bed she shares with Daddy, and lays me in the middle. I am a buffer, a bunker, a sandbag. I am ten years old. My body is no longer that of a child-girl. Sujata, my best friend at school, is small and bony. But this trunk of a body has sprouted buds which flop onto my sides as I lie on my back, staring at the white ceiling. The bed is a river of soundless tears soaking into sheets. Daddy switches off the lights. Daddy comes to bed wearing only his underpants. He smells of vomit and Goan lime pickle, his legs are hairy, his pants curve over a flouncing bulge. He slides into bed. His hand glides over me and reaches out to touch Mummy. She is having none of it. She pushes his hand away. The river is in full spate. I am afraid to lie next to him. His body is prickly against my skin. My chin no longer lodges into his neck. My legs no longer hook onto his hips. How do I fit into his body now? I move closer to Mummy. Daddy moves away from me. He is negotiating the space between us. He stopped negotiating with Mummy some time ago; their marriage is an arid dust bowl which grows nothing but discontent.

2

Sisterhood of Swans

The summer I turn fifteen, Daddy moves out. I don't understand why he is abandoning me. I tug at his shirt and wrap my arms around him, but he leaves anyway.

Months later, he invites me to spend the weekend at his new home. He's living on the other side of Horton, a small village on the hem of north London. My parents have only ever known Horton as their home in Britain. Mummy was already pregnant with me when they landed at Heathrow Airport on a cold December day in 1989; two Goans looking for a new life. Horton lies not far from Heathrow. Horton blurs the boundary between London and the great expanse of the country that exists outside of it. In the summer, cob horses graze in the open field which backs on to Otterfield Lane. It's hard to imagine otters this far out from deep river, but they must have come up the sleeve of the marshy bank at one time because places and families carry names that mean something even when everything else alters course.

When I arrive, Daddy's standing in front of a stump of a house springing forth from feathering tufts of grass, enclosed in a pale blue fence with its serrated mouth bleeding berries. He draws me into a circle of arms. I am even further away from him than I was when he lived with us. He is a stranger; a soft-bellied, smiling stranger. The type you meet in corner-shops.

His new love-interest comes out to meet me.

'This is Martha,' he says, pulling her close to him.

She's wearing the taut smile she must have worked on for a week. She's a thin English woman with coarse hair. This doesn't look like something Daddy has fallen into arse-backwards. This has the whiff of careful planning, and Daddy's protective hand on her swollen belly confirms that. We are all connected now by an invisible wire which passes from my ankle through to Daddy's heart and into Martha's belly. But Daddy is severed from Mummy. I feel a metal cutter clipping away at the wiring holding us all together.

I trail my trolley bag into the house. Inside, the house is violent with noise from the TV. There's a boy of about seventeen sitting on the sofa in the small living room crowded with mismatched furniture. It occurs to me that this isn't Daddy's home at all. That he's in fact living in Martha's home.

The boy looks so much like Martha that he can only be Martha's son. He's all dangly arms and legs. I look at him more closely. He's quite beautiful with a long, oval face unscarred by puberty. Whatever little hair had shown up on his face by way of a beard and moustache has been shaved off, leaving behind stubble which makes him look almost manly. I see a large Adam's apple bobbing on his scrawny neck. His eyes are fixed on the TV, his hands are manoeuvring a retro joystick. Occasionally, triumph registers on his face.

Daddy plops himself on the sofa, next to the boy.

'Daniel, this is my daughter Anna-Marie,' he says.

Daniel nods in the direction of the TV, unwilling to break gaze. There's a victory achieved on the lighted screen, which makes him jump up in his seat. He slaps Daddy's thigh. I notice Daddy inch his leg away. Daniel is trying to negotiate space in my Daddy's life, just as I am, only Daddy has no place for him. Daniel and I belong to no one. I make a silent promise to myself: I'll never leave the father of my child. I'll stay. Whatever it takes, I'll stay till their tiny arms no longer feel the need to wrap themselves around a father.

Later in the day, Daddy is on the sofa, his legs propped up on the armrest, watching football. Daniel is watching the game with him.

'Shower?' Daddy asks, seeing me walk towards the bathroom, pink towel and shampoo bottle in hand. I nod.

'Remember how you used to fight me when I would scrub you?' He laughs into his beer can.

I stare blankly. Daniel looks at me, a clown-smile painted on his face. I don't want Daniel to know that the man on the sofa—my father—had scrubbed me. That he had prised open my unwilling hands and legs, and scrubbed off the caked playground mud with a pink scrub.

'Someone has to take care of you,' he would say, hauling me into his arms and lowering my body into the tub. He'd kneel by the tub, watching the water turn soapy, then he'd leave me to it.

When I'd told Sujata at school that Daddy bathed me every evening, she'd said, 'Eew. Why?'

But I wasn't soured on my Daddy as Sujata was on hers. Sujata, at six, planned to run away from home as soon as she'd saved up a pound.

'Why can't your mum do it?' Sujata had persisted,

her tiny teeth biting into an apple. Sujata hated fruit but had to eat her share at carpet-time or Miss Folan would make her sit in the corner. Sujata hated a lot of things: dogs, bees, darkness.

'She goes out.'

'Where does she go?'

'To catch butterflies.'

'With a net?'

'I don't know.'

'I wish my Daddy would catch butterflies. But he never goes out.'

I'd felt nothing in those days. Neither shame nor guilt. I'd lain in that bathtub of ceramic pink, naked, shimmering and silken, the rippling water conniving, half-truths raging and rising like so many moons tossed into the sky. I'd gathered all the storms in that house, thundering and striking, bolts of lightning flashing and flaring between Daddy and Mummy, and sunk deeper into the water. But Daddy had always fished me out, towelled me dry, and put me to bed. Our bodies fit into each other perfectly, my little hands curled around his neck, my knees tucked into his belly, my chin nuzzled into his chest. He was big and warm, like a gentle giant, and he made me feel safe.

The next morning, Daniel is sitting at the kitchen table, his fingers nimble on a Nintendo console. I pull back a chair to sit next to him.

'D'you like Pokémon?' he asks.

'No.'

'Where'd you go to school?'

His eyes are snakes slithering over my breasts. I push my breasts further out. They are almost touching his elbow now.

'Grover's Green.'

'Why so far?'

'It's a grammar school.'

'St Mary's?'

'Yah.'

'Posh then, innit?'

'Not really. It's just a school.'

'Annie tried to get into a grammar. Couldn't.'

'Who's Annie?'

'Me and Annie hang out.'

My shorts ride up my chicken-skin thighs exposing expanses of flesh. My knuckles are red from clenching the sides of my chair. I want to ask him about things—about football, about bikes, about Gameboy—but my tongue sits thick and heavy in my mouth, wallowing in a pool of self-loathing. Under the table, hidden from view, is a world of half-formed desires. I am no longer Daddy's little girl.

Daniel licks his rhubarb-red mouth, and stands up. His eyes are cloudy with want. He's just a boy. Not yet a man. But already he knows that he holds the upper hand. That he'll always hold the upper hand with women.

'Will you be back next week?'

He's standing so close to me now that I can feel his breath on my neck. Under his X-Men T-shirt I discern a cage of antlers. His skin smells of the musk of his species. He's stronger than he looks. He will grow up to be a fine breeding bull.

I say, 'I don't know.'

But I do know.

Saturday next, I am on the doorstep of that ugly house yet again. Daddy elbows the door open. We're going to drop this off at Barnardo's, he says, holding a box of books. Books he no longer needs in his new life. Books which had been such a big part of his old life. Books Martha, who has slid out of the shadows behind him, has probably never read. He's out of breath, his stomach bulging over his belt. Make yourself at home. Daniel's in his room, he says, turning to look at me over his shoulder before he shuts the door.

The house is a monastery of quiet rooms and cold floors. The long shaft of afternoon light leaking from Daniel's half-closed door beckons me. I knock on its paint-peeling front.

'Come in,' Daniel says. 'You're back.'

Standing at the foot of the bed, I nod. He's wearing shorts and a T-shirt, his head propped on a tower of pillows, his blackened knees flexed, his fingers on a console. His legs are scrawnier than I thought they'd be, and I wonder now if I'm ready to see his scrawny body naked. He's just a boy. A stupid boy. Not yet a man who might be warm, gentle and safe. I sit on the edge of the bed, my eyes on the summer-leafing sheets.

'Pokémon again?'

'Um-hm.'

I make to go, but his body has sprung into motion, and leapt right next to where I'm standing. He holds my wrist in a firm grip, hurting me. I don't understand his need for power; I'm humiliated by it. I squirm. He lets go, leaving a ring of white on my skin. My insides are rattling winds and crackling trees. I'm acutely aware Daniel is different from me. He is what Mummy calls 'not our type.' Mummy is a poet. She is forever trying to capture the zeitgeist of her times, her butterflies, she calls them. She's raised me to be liberal, but Mummy's mouth is so cruel about Daddy's new family, that the boundaries of acceptance have blurred within me. The snobbery of class and breeding now raises itself like a forbidding nationalist monument. And yet a warm desire seeps through my pride, spreading to my body. I move awkwardly toward him.

Daniel's lips curl, his tongue twists, his teeth gird upon my mouth. His hands reach under my blouse and unhook the metal clasp which holds my breasts in lacy half-cups. My breasts pour into his palms. His fingers graze my nipples. I try to focus on the wall behind him. I inhale deeply of the sweat beading on his neck. But it's no good. I clamp shut my thighs. Inexperienced as I am, I know that my legs should be falling away, that I should be guiding him into my joins and dips. Sujata and I, we've talked about this so many times, it should be like answering an exam.

'Fuck, fuck, fuck. Are you a virgin?' he yells, as if in pain.

My eyes are tearing up. He pushes himself away. He's islanded amidst the paisley leaf bedding. He has no interest in being my 'first.' We are not friends to patch over this with forgiveness. We are not lovers, to be patient with each other's failings. We are strangers at a mountain impasse manoeuvring past our inexperience. I hook my bra. He returns to playing Pokémon.

In the morning, Martha is in the kitchen, a steel knife in hand, its butt pressed into her palm, its edge cutting through the pale pink of sinew. She wields the knife with precision, letting the blood bleed onto her hand. The meat is diced methodically until all that remains of the clod is bone. She looks at me as I sit at the table.

'Where's Daddy?' I ask.

'Out in the garden,' she says, nodding in the direction of the open window.

My heart is a rock wedged in my throat.

'And Daniel?'

'He's spending the day at Annie's. Down the road. Best of friends, those two are. Always with each other. Childhood sweethearts, you might call them.'

She knows. Just as every woman knows. We belong to the sisterhood of swans, seeking to pair for life, curving our necks to entwine with the perfect mate. Only we seldom find them. Our species is doomed to disappointment.

Outside sits a granite London sky penetrated by red roofs. Daddy is hunched over a patch of green. I want to crawl into him, cradle my head in the crook of his arm, fasten myself to his chest. But he's there, weeding another woman's back garden and smiling at her from where he's crouched, ankle-deep in sod.

3

Ghosts of Abandoned Women

The fogs of London are clearing and upon me arrive the streets, faster and faster, until I can see its sea of people swelling and unswelling, and white gulls moving in a floating file across a cleft of horizon carved into cloud. I am alone on a sloop of familiar strangers. In the pale pond of autumnal light, I see the ghost of an abandoned woman skimming the scalloped skirts of wedding dresses in a shop-window. The ghost stares back at me. She is a tall, plumpish ghost of twenty-six: her arms, her breasts, her buttocks, are all plumpish; her face is plumpish, with curious eyes and framed with shoulder-length hair. Men find her attractive. You're a healthy size, they say, with a healthy appetite. You're what women should look like, they tell her. Only, the ghost has never believed herself to be attractive.

I watch Sujata emerge from the ebbing crowd at the bus stop. She crosses the road to avoid a boy on roller-skates. She crosses it back again to avoid the berry-fruiting brambles. In the brambles are bees which might sting, and Sujata is afraid of bees. She meets me at the worn-looking bridal shop which is offering discounts for the fashionable '2016 Autumn Bride'. A dog on a lead pads too close to her, sniffing at her shoes. She stiffens, looking helplessly at me.

'Get your dog out of the way, Mister,' I say to the

dog-walker, who looks at us, glassy-eyed with age, and annoyed by this unexpected glare of hate.

'Your friend's afraid of dogs? Fear is learnt. Teach her to overcome it.'

'You don't know a fucking thing about my friend. Get your ugly mutt away from her or I'll kick its face in.'

The dog-walker recoils as if from a fire. I'm convinced the dog's replaced everything missing in his life—love, companionship, respect. I feel sorry for him, sorry for how limiting his life has turned out to be, but my principal loyalty will always be to Sujata. I owe her that much, for all that I've taken from her.

'Come on, Locky. Let's leave the crazy ladies alone.' He pulls the lead tightly, and guides the dog past us.

Sujata is relieved. We fall into easy step; she, a good head taller than me. I put my hand in my jeans pocket and fish out the telephone number Sanjay had slipped me at the Six Bells pub. She looks at me, hopelessly disappointed.

'Do you know anything about this man? Is Sanjay even his real name?' she asks, linking her arm in mine and stubbing out her cigarette. I wave the smoke away, refusing to be a passive participant in her self-harm.

'What's to know? Indian man born to Punjabi parents. They came here in the Seventies, bought a corner-shop and sent their first-spawned to college.'

'So that makes him what? Fifty? Charming.'

'Don't be silly. He's just forty.'

'Isn't that too old for you?' You're not looking for a daddy-figure, are you?'

'What if I am?'

Sujata rolls her eyes.

'I bet his mother told him to work twice as hard to be half as successful as a white man, *beta*,' she says, mimicking an Indian accent.

'And he dyed his hair blond and wore track pants, just to fit in. Until he discovered he could be his own man. See, I know all there is to know.'

'He sounds like a wanker.'

'He probably is. A wanker plus plus.'

But I have no idea who Sanjay really is, and I'm peddling stereotype here. Every face bears a story: crack open the surface, rend the skin, expose the kernel.

'So you think I shouldn't see him?'

'You're going to do exactly as you please. You always do.'

'I value your advice.'

'And then you do the exact opposite.'

'I'm very impulsive.'

Sujata laughs. 'That you are.'

We turn the corner on Old Glebe Road; on the High Street is the Horton fish and chip shop which hardly has any customers. Mr Burrage spends his day at the door cursing all the Indian curry houses and chasing away the school kids who hang around there smoking weed, not buying anything.

'If the devil had a net for the lot of you…Get out of here.' He shoos them away with a baseball bat. They disperse for a few minutes, then form again like a whirring murmuration of starlings.

Last night, Sanjay had bought me blond beer with big head and licked the foam off my lips. His body was flat, hard, used to common labour, but he was not inelegant.

He spoke politely, the way those who take their state schooling seriously, often do.

He said, 'Can I ask you something?'

'What?'

'Have you been to the back alley?'

'I'm guessing you have.'

'Frequently.'

'Is it worth visiting?'

'Yes. With me as your guide.'

He put his hands on my buttocks and led me behind the Six Bells. The air smelt of roast pork and baked potatoes, and a bright street light shone in my face. I rubbed the light out of my eyes and saw other couples there, women in fishnet stockings and big blonde hair, pinned onto men with long, thick overcoats. The cold night air had turned us all into smoking dragons clustering in corners. I closed my eyes and let his hand slip up my skirt, his fingers finding the fleshy mound. His face soft, his breathing nasally, his eyes watery, he took my breath away. He was the liminal light, the blur, the riff, the cliff, the everything that hangs in the balance. I thought of Daddy. I haven't seen Daddy in ten years but I think of him every time I'm with someone new.

Sujata and I reach Doctor Yates' office. We climb the spiral stairs together, careful not to be noticed.

'Wait here,' she whispers, squeezing my hand.

'You'll be fine. Don't worry. I'll be right outside.'

I wait anxiously for her on the landing. Across the street, Jassie from Bollywood Style Salon paces the pavement, mobile stuck to ear, a stream of Punjabi flowing from her reddened lips, erratically punctuated with 'Bluddy bastard.'

A nose-ringed, blonde girl from Mattie's Floral Bouquets comes out, and gently tapping Jassie on the shoulder, kisses her on the lips. She borrows a cigarette and takes a long drag. Jassie whispers in the blonde girl's ear and they wave out to me from the smoke cloud which envelops them, billowing upwards into the ramshackle shop signs. Then stamping out her cigarette, the blonde girl makes rude hand gestures, and shouts out, 'Oi, what you looking at, dipshit, we ain't gay or nuttin', like you and your pal.' They laugh, and retreat into their shops. I stand awkwardly, rooted to the spot. It's not uncommon in London to be confronted, unexpectedly, by ugliness. But surely not to be abetted in this sorry act by someone I know, however peripherally. Why did Jassie laugh at me? The sun comes up just then and the street brightens.

4

Nights are for Hunting

I meet Sanjay again at the Six Bells. He's wearing corduroy pants and a white shirt; a brown Adonis amidst tall, blonde sea nymphs. There is about him a certain tenderness which comes from being held always within a circle of love, but also a certain hardness which I sense takes advantage of the attention he receives. I notice at once that he has a roving eye but I don't feel any ownership over him as yet. I push through the thicket of beauties and perch myself on a high-top chair. I don't like pubs with their dart boards, damp carpets and tattooed ladettes downing pints. But I'm not so alone or alien sitting next to Sanjay.

'Hello, my passionflower,' I say.

He leans over and kisses me on the lips. 'Play your cards right and you'll see some passion tonight, sweetheart. What you having?'

'I'll have a pint.'

It's warm inside the pub; a few football fans burst through the door, with club scarves wrapped tightly around their necks, chanting, 'England. England, England,' swept away on a tidal wave of nationalism, unable to break from a siege of oneness and a feeling of accomplishment which they personally have nothing to do with. They scatter around the bar ordering draft beer and munching on peanuts.

'I'd tear the ref's head off, if I could,' says one.

'Yeah, I'd hang the goalie by the balls,' says another one.

They link arms and form a chain, singing, 'Can you score? Can you score? Can you score a goal for us?'

Their voices grow loud and threatening, their jeers ricochet off the pea-green walls.

Sanjay and I disentangle from the crowd around the bar, and have our dinner by the fireside: chicken tandoori biryani for him and lamb chops for me. The sprigs of rosemary smell like Christmas but the lamb is chewy and thick with fat.

'Are you a footie fan?' I ask Sanjay.

'Don't know the first thing about the game. I don't care for it at all.'

We are swallowed whole by the chanting chorus of sports nationalism just then, by the sour-smelling beer, by the blackness of a dense sky over the northern hemisphere. Before us lies the wide chasm of an England we can't cross and the inescapability of an ethnic alienation we can't deny. We're imposters at the gate, and we know it. Sanjay and I are held together by an instant primal kinship based on the imagined intimacy of all such kinship. In the fireside flames, I see how I've contrived historical narratives to form an alliance with Sanjay, to create a shadow of solidarity which I think I can embrace, but which I sense will collapse when reality intrudes. Sanjay talks about things that make me laugh, that spin in my head, that bubble up in my stomach, that tingle up my spine. The serious me, the whimsical me, the accomplished me, the time-worn me, all reborn, not of substance but of illusion.

On our way home, we get lost and slip into an unlit

alley. A black cat crosses the street. Black cats have an unsavoury reputation. Black cats belong to women with pointy hats and brooms, black cats belong to women waiting in flats with flat-packed furniture, for love to arrive. To want love is to be needy. To pursue love is to be weak. It makes other women pity you. It makes men take advantage of you. It makes Indian parents ashamed of you. By God, I am needy.

It's dark in the rain-washed alley. Caterwauling black cats loom over its narrow belly winding its way deeper into darkness. Sanjay steps on cat shit but that doesn't stop him. He unbuttons my blouse and unclasps my bra. His large hands slope along my breasts, his scudding mouth suckles me. I trace the eyelets running down his shirt, the constrained contours of his corduroys. I want to make him moan like men are known to moan, like cats are known to yowl, like winds are known to whistle. I want to make him happy like men are known to be happy when they've had a good day at work, come home to a good meal, find reruns of Jeremy Clarkson driving through a crowded street ranting about foreign cars. A skittish cat flies in our face and lands at our feet. We withdraw from the unborn dream that holds us together, interrupted by this cat-drone patrolling the dark. We douse our madness with the mundane business of getting home. At the bus stop, we wait under the watery blur of moonlight. A *Metro News* is wedged in the steel joins of the fibreglass rain shelter. Sanjay unwedges it and glances at an ink-stained story about homelessness.

He says, 'I wish we could do something about this.'

He's a bit of all right, I think. Should I invite him home? I've only met him twice and good Indian girls don't invite men home. I live in a studio flat with a soiled, single mattress spread on the floor. The snout-nosed bus splashes a pee-coloured puddle. I panic.

Turning to him, I say, 'Should we go to your place?'

I watch Sanjay sleeping in the airless room. His left hand is upright, the fingers curved into a stiff claw. If I'd known him better I'd know what the claw meant. Long-time lovers are privileged. They know how to decode somnambulatory desires. For itinerant lovers, nights are for hunting under a moon, its yellowed entrails hanging in hollows of hills. Nights are for prising the self from the shadow. Sagged over a velveteen blanket, sleeping on sunless dreams, balled foetal, cracked toes curling, railed in by Sanjay's arm, I recoil. Definitions construct on lilac linen sheets. Frames too small to fit into frameworks of womanhood: I want, I desire, I am vulnerable, I am lonely, I am girl, I am kite, I am kite flying, I am leaf falling, I am fish swimming, I am fowl flouncing, I am fool faking, I am woman floundering. I am all things at all times. I am many things with many needs.

In the morning I put the wine bottle back in the fridge and wipe the table clean. I wash the glasses in the sink and put away the knives. This kitchen is stamped with the smells of ancient recipes: neatly labelled jars of turmeric, coriander, cloves, cinnamon, fennel, poppy and star anise. I respect the space which contains a certain unknown presence. I wonder about this unknown presence, what she might be like. In my mind, I give her a generic name and so a generic face and a generic body floats into my imagination, and in the conjuring, I am better than her in every way. From the kitchen, I watch Sanjay asleep, weighed down dead as a pig. His lies have knocked the air right out of me. He is just like Daddy.

5

The Waiting Room

I spend the morning at the Horton Medical Centre, sitting next to an old lady. The once-black hair is a fluff of white. It has curled up. It is a mat of curl around her lined face. She sits unaware of my existence and me unmindful of hers except for the one quick glance I steal. Then our worlds dissolve and go their separate ways to heal privately the pain which brings us here to this precise point in time. Later, I wonder about the woman and what might have brought her to the doctor's office, our worlds so close that they almost touched. It could have been any number of things: diabetes, arthritis, cancer. What if it was cancer? Is the finality of existence the end of life or the end of an encounter? After all, people cease to exist if they are no longer part of our lives. But what if they ebb and flow in and out of our consciousness, like Daddy? What are we to make of them, then?

London is built in such a way that we all cease to exist within minutes of meeting. London's worlds are tributaries running parallel to each other. English, Irish, Polish, Punjabi, Sindhi, Goans, Yemenis, Somalis are isolated pools of humanity swirling and eddying at bus stops and traffic signals, detached and disparate. There were parts of London called Chhota Punjab once but now the Goans have a strong presence here. Righteous ringing of Hail Marys can be heard from every Catholic church from Ealing to Southall. Mummy says we should wish some of them *boas festas* next Christmas Mass at St Catherine's Church.

The waiting room is white with a phalanx of plastic chairs from which rise wraiths when their numbers are called, to meet their fate. In the corner is a frump of a fir tree with dusty red baubles and fairy lights blinking dull Christmas cheer, and above it, on the wall, is a muted TV set with 'breaking news' headlines about a terrorist attack on a Christmas market in Germany. But the room is thick with its own preoccupations of seasonal viruses and hacking coughs, and barely notices the flashing images of ambulances carrying away dismembered bodies. Horton is distilled into seclusion and all those things that happen to London, the terrorist attacks, the knife crime, the smash-n-grab heists, seem so far away even though we live on its blistering edge. At Horton we believe nothing will touch us.

Farida Ahmed, please proceed to room No. 8. Farida Ahmed, room No. 8 please.

The voice over the public address system is synthetic. Farida Ahmed's fate is decided by an automaton. In room no. 8 awaits a doctor who will not know Farida Ahmed's mother or father or if they suffered from the same ailment Farida Ahmed suffers from today. The doctor will peer into a computer and Farida Ahmed's medical history will appear on the lighted screen. Farida Ahmed is a computer entry, an Excel sheet, a past prescription, a current address. Farida Ahmed exists only on screen and once she leaves the doctor's room all traces of her will evaporate and be replaced by the next name located by date of birth. Nobody cares about family histories. We are all powdered into numbers and statistics.

Mummy sits beside me blank-eyed and barren of emotion. She's beautifully made up in stiff, blue Marks & Spencer's slacks and a floral silk blouse, the sartorial choice of fashionable Goan ladies in London.

'Don't fidget,' she says, 'you're always fidgeting.'

I stop at once my restless foot-tapping.

'Why are you always so fidgety, impatience is something you've inherited from your good-for-nothing father.' She jabs the javelin where she knows it will hurt.

Mother Kali-Durga: Giver of life, collector of tears, interpreter of dreams, prophet of hope, destroyer of self-esteem. Mummy is paradox, conundrum, the two-faced Janus: Mummy knows the innermost parts of me. She is a compendium of cold wisdom which some inner voice instructs me to revere as sacred. She is the intractable rock upon which I lean. Mummy is good, Mummy is cruel. Mummy with her tongue lashings is terrifying and I'm afraid of her. She explains her cruelty as character-building or as a joke. She doesn't understand that shit in a house shifts until it settles on the littlest person. She doesn't realise the trauma of her marriage has grown muscle memory in me. It has sunk into the bark of my being and now snaps and scrapes at will. Her sworn oath that she would rather die than hurt me is the empty hollow of a tree. I wonder if every child ever born who has wriggled through the birth canal with the umbilical cord intact has had this relationship with their mother: bound by blood and bone, fuelled by rage.

Akina Kamau please proceed to room No. 10. Akina Kamau, room No. 10 please.

In place of the white-haired lady is a frilly-frocked, watery-eyed girl playing a Christmas song on her mobile, without headphones. She's making the knot in my stomach tighten even more. I feel nauseous.

'Have you spoken to Sanjay?' Mummy asks.

'No.'

'Where does he work?'

'At Tesco's.'

'The Horton Tesco?'

I nod.

'Is he the one then? *Le grand amour*? They're not our kind of people but you went sniffing around there, and that's that.'

I avoid her gaze. As a Catholic Goan, Mummy's rhetoric is always directed sequentially in a precise order at: anyone she thinks is lower class; anyone who's Indian and not Goan (because 1961, of course, Nehru and invasion); and anyone who doesn't read the same books as her. Mummy doesn't acknowledge her Indian-ness. 'I'm a Portuguese-Goan,' she says to people who enquire about her peculiar surname. 'I am not any one thing. I was born on the crossroads of seafaring histories.'

'All Goans hate Indians,' she tells me frequently.

'No Mummy, you're the only Indian-hating Indian I know,' I reply.

By every definition of the word, Mummy lives on the periphery of Horton. On the edge of being brown. On the circumference of white. Her food and music never Indian enough. Her culture and Christianity never European enough. The *kutcha-butcha* of Indian society. The 'neither fish nor fowl' of the west. A mongrel. And nobody likes mongrels.

Mummy won't be distracted, and after a while, she retorts: 'It's tragic that your generation believes in a soulmate.'

'And yours didn't?'

'My generation made everything possible for yours.'

'In what way?'

'We were the first generation to take men to bed without a wedding ring on our finger.'

'We'll mail you a letter of thanks.'

She ignores my biliousness.

'We held out on marriage for as long as we could, built our careers instead, made something of ourselves.'

'How is that any different from me?'

'We didn't believe in soulmates. We were pragmatists. This soulmate-rollmate business belongs to your generation.'

She crosses her legs and uncrosses them, she shifts in her chair roiling with ambitions turned rancid. She dreams of cocktail parties, little black dresses, vape in hand, holding forth on Ted Hughes and Sylvia Plath: 'Darling, their marriage was such a celebration of combined genius, don't you think? I know, I know, it drove Plath to suicide but she was disturbed. That's what accounts for her genius, no?' Mummy is the embodiment of modernity, a woman way before her time. She's also a bastion of parochial Goan prudery who, growing up, made sure I never wore mini-skirts and sleeveless tops.

'Frankly, I feel betrayed,' she says, 'I feel like you've thrown me under the bus. You've grown up so needy of male attention. You have no sense of self-worth without having a man in your life.'

I twist the edge of my belt.

'I'm sorry I'm a disappointment. Maybe if you had held on to your man, I wouldn't be like this.'

Her eyes are unsmiling.

I'm in a white room with fairy lights and failed

expectations all around. I feel the urge to damage Mummy some more.

'Did you have a feeling that Daddy would leave you?'

'All sensible women know their men will leave them eventually. One way or another, they will betray us.'

'Really?'

'They are dead to us long before they leave us for their stinking whores.'

I am taken aback by Mummy's deep sense of disgust at the male species.

'Is that why you want me to believe in this great fraternity of self-sufficient women? Women who think men are toxic.'

'Stop being smug.'

'What is it you call yourself? The Travelling Sisterhood of Unfulfilled Desire?'

'That's rubbish.'

'Is it?

'There's solidarity to be found amongst women of substance.'

'I never said there wasn't, Mummy. But what I need, what my body needs, what my soul needs is something different. I'm not going to let you make me feel small for wanting the things I want.'

'You mean you need a man. What is that called? Anti-feminism? Post-feminism?

'I know your kind of feminism, Mummy.'

'Which is?'

'Idolise women you don't know and dump on those you do. Your kind of feminism is always on the lookout for us lesser women.'

'I don't dump on women.'

'Yes, you do. You dump on women you feel are weak and who don't subscribe to your way of thinking. You're a bully.'

'You're bowing to convention. Something we fought so hard to overcome. You're taking the cause of feminism several steps back.'

'I am not an *ism*, Mummy.'

'You're a traitor, Anna-Marie.'

'Well, don't sound so bitter or anything. You really must get out and start dating again. Before you completely shrivel up.' I want her to hurt. Despite the bravado, I know she still misses Daddy.

'I'm not going to turn into that sad, lonely middle-aged woman trying to flirt.'

'Try seducing in the dark. They won't see your turkey neck that way.'

'Laugh now, you'll get there soon enough. Besides, all the great loves of our life belong to our youth.' She says this with a certain wistfulness which makes me uneasy. What is she trying to tell me? Is it possible Mummy is being prescient?

I turn my attention back to the little girl sitting next to me, wanting to wrench her mobile away from her and smash it to the floor. I say, 'Hello, who's looking after you, then?'

The girl leans into the man on her side and says, 'Daddy.'

I look up at the man; he's on his mobile reading messages, and beside him is another man nervously shuffling his feet, and one further away, in a white shirt, staring vacantly ahead, listening intently to the names being called out. In this offering of men which

Horton throws up, I still hope to find a soulmate somehow. Mummy thinks it tragic that I carry the idea of a soulmate, harvested from every book I've ever read by Paulo Coelho. At some point, I know I'm going to outgrow Paulo Coelho, it's becoming difficult to believe in the infinite wisdom of the universe directing my life to glorious fulfilment. But not today. Today, I still believe that trajectories will lead to unforeseen outcomes in collusion with the horned-unicorn of the universe.

Anna-Marie Souza please proceed to room No. 9, Anna-Marie Souza room No. 9 please.

6

Guilt and the Light Traveller

Black-winged bird on birch tree; a clumsy cloud lurches for the sky. The dead of winter arrives in its coat of white. Battalions of fog banks rise in the night. The radiators hum songs of a summer revival. I feel the cold on my face; the night is cruel and callous settling in the corners of my room. I am eyeless in this economy of light, listening to the words asshole and fuck looping from nearby neighbourhood windows. Somewhere is a Beatles song being played.

I've left several messages for Sanjay but have not heard back from him in a week. It's late Friday evening when he calls and asks me to meet him at his house. We've met often at the Six Bells' rent-by-hour rooms (and the landlady sensing continued custom always gives us the same room), but only once at his house—the first time. The knot tightens. I leave my flat under cover of darkness. I see a sad-eyed dog cross the road near the 'Red Squirrels, Drive Slowly' signpost. He looks at me, bushy-tailed and sympathetic. Dogs understand. They know what it is to be lonely for their owners. The No. 222 bus is lit from within, a moving beacon of fluorescent hope travelling through Horton.

'Are you going past Belcose Road?' I ask the driver.

'Near enough, Miss.'

'Will you let me know when we're close.'

'Will do, Miss.'

'Thank you, Driver.'

The bus is empty except for a young West Indian lad in the front seat with his headphones on, and Jassie on the back seat sprawled its full length with her feet propped up against the windows, the fading blonde streaks in her hair making her head look like a wicker basket. She's talking loudly into her mobile.

'Bluddy bastard, didn't pay again this month. Mine ones need shoes for school, mine ones go without food, does he care?' I hear her say.

I wonder if Jassie is married or seeing someone and if that 'bluddy bastard' is the someone. She glares at me then and juts her chin out, in recognition. I smile at her. She puts her phone in her pocket and gives me the middle finger. I wonder what I've done to be despised by Jassie. I wonder if Jassie with her red varnish nails will rip my skin out the next time I'm lying naked in a dirty cubicle at Bollywood Style Salon. Will she exercise her wanton power when she's standing poised over me, hot-wax knife in hand, saying, 'Spread leg, please.' I turn my head and gaze into the bottomless black of the night trying to make out street names.

A few minutes later, I get off the bus and walk to Belcose Road. A cat darts into the holly hedgerow when a car pulls out of a driveway. There are no streetlamps here. The night is silent and solemn with promise. In the distance, I can hear the hoarse cry of foxes and I feel instinctively a clamp of fear for all the defenceless creatures who hide in the bushes. I arrive at House No. 9, the house where I must secret a space for myself. Sanjay opens the door wearing white kurta pyjamas. He looks older than he does in corduroys. His hair, left untended, is greying at the edges and his eyes are more burdened than usual. Guilt is not suited to the light traveller. It weighs heavy.

He says, 'Come in.'

I walk the path which curves into a room, into light, into a future. I possess nothing other than the utility of my body. Layer me, cover the deprivations of my past, predict the potential of my future. Between now and tomorrow, lies possibility.

The first time, he'd hurried me into the bedroom but now, today, I have more time to unearth the stories his house will reveal to me. I gravitate quickly to the bookcase in the living room. There on the shelf are curious titles: books on management and trains, and travels to dusty Indian towns. These reveal nothing, as an Orwell or Rushdie or even a Deepak Chopra might have done. These are shelved clichés and petty vanities nestling between bookends. There are bottles of whiskey sheltering on shelves, a wide-screen TV with surround sound speakers, an ugly Formica cabinet with wooden carved elephants and a marble Taj Mahal, a batik of a blue-faced Krishna above a dusty, disused fireplace, and a small gold cup announcing the winner of the Indian Gymkhana Cricket Tournament. On the wall, is a framed and garlanded picture of a couple.

The house looks as if it's been transplanted from the faceless commuter towns of Reading or Watford to which well-heeled Indian doctors, pharmacists, ophthalmologists and IT engineers move as soon as they can afford better postcodes. Once there, they form small communities of other successful Indians whose kids all go to grammar school and Maths tuition classes, whose vacations include Malé and Malta, and whose Saturdays are spent learning yoga, playing badminton and visiting each other.

There is nothing here that says this house wants to be part of London. This is a house in denial about where it belongs, it's a withdrawal into a proud conservatism which Asian lives flaunt, but also want to escape. I point to the picture and ask: 'Who are they?'

'My parents.'

'They live in London?'

'They died in a flood, in Punjab.'

'I'm sorry.'

'It wasn't your fault.'

'No, I just meant…'

'I know what you meant.'

'How did you get here?'

'On the back of a lorry.'

'You having a laugh?'

'Kiran Mamaji adopted me as a child. I came here when I was seven. I hated going to school. Imagine being the kid from India in Eighties Britain. Look, I don't want to talk about it.'

Sanjay stands behind me as he always does, a move I recognise as a precursor to our lovemaking. I can feel his breathing burning my neck. His silence slides between my ribs, clawing at my heart.

Conversations with Sanjay are desultory rivers flowing in starts and spurts. Some futile attempt is made just before our lovemaking: 'Have you had a bite?', 'How was traffic?', 'Any plans for the weekend?', and then as if on cue the guilt kicks in as soon as the body breaks and the spasms recede. He tosses out of bed, makes some excuse and disappears hastily, half-forgetting to shut the door behind him. I lie sprawled on soiled sheets, my arms aching to hold him, my tongue thickened with words left unspoken. One time, I tried to shame him and asked to leave some money on the mantlepiece. He'd smirked and exited twice as fast. Tonight's going to be different.

He puts his arms around me; then breaks away. He rifles through his pocket and retrieves a plastic pouch containing what seem like clumps of crushed tea leaves. My stomach turns at the sight of it and I feel nausea wash over me. He puts his hand out, wagging the pouch, then unseals it and inhales deeply of its smell. He asks, 'Have you ever smoked weed?'

This *is* different.

'I've had huge smoke rings blown in my face and I've inhaled a good bit but I've never smoked any.'

'Would you like to?'

I think momentarily how good it would be to experience total surrender with Sanjay. To dissolve into oblivion and find everything he says to be infinitely profound. But some cold clarity cuts through my brain. Men who plan a future with you don't offer you recreational drugs.

I shake my head.

He shrugs and says, 'Suit yourself.' He unfurls a rolling paper, lines it with the dried leaves, attaches a filter tip and draws in its substance. A plume of smoke blows into my face and I hold my breath not wanting to inhale.

He takes my hand into his hairy paw and leads me

towards the arc of light coming from a nearby room. We feel our way through the demi-darkness, our bodies limp with surrender. This tumultuous tempest, this wretched dram of desire, we drink of deeply.

In the bedroom, her unseen spectre inhabits the neatly piled stacks of *Stardust* magazines, trapped in the pleats of floral curtains, bunched on the bed with *khadi* cushions, clinging to the cottons on the wall hanger. I sense a wholesomeness carried in trunks from India. Some alien tongue, some pebbles from a beach, some powdered spice, some bright beads, some precious books, must have travelled with her in the hope of starting a new life. Now all she has is an orderly existence in this room, a world carefully bordered between him and her, and oceaned by quiet indifference. But the life of his wife belongs to the marshlands of my imagination without any grounding in reality. I am vaguely aware of her as one is of blurry, faceless people, but I have no real interest in her. My only concern is for myself.

Our desire drained, the fury of darkness is upon me, and I lie abandoned, seeking refuge under the duvet, filling the space left hollow by her, carrying the cyclone wreckage of ruined lives. The knot tightens and tightens.

When he wakes up, I mean to tell him what I've been holding back, but I ask him instead why he cheats on his wife.

'I was never going to be faithful,' he says.

'Why?'

'When I was about twenty-four, I fell in love with a beautiful Parsi girl. She was a great girl. A really great girl. We had great sex. I loved her a lot.'

'And?'

'Couldn't marry her. Wasn't allowed to by her father. I just knew I'd never be faithful after that.'

'That's rubbish.'

'What is? That I wasn't allowed to marry her?'

'That excuse you just cooked up. Jesus, why are men such dicks? Grow up.'

'You're all grown up are you, sleeping around with married men?'

'You disgust me.'

'Back at you with knobs on.'

'You're full of deceitful self-justifications.'

He shrugs: 'If you're going to psychoanalyse me, I might as well lie down.' He stretches himself on the bed, smiling at me dismissively, scratching my skin as he pulls me to him, but I yank away. I notice how yellow and hooked his toenails are. Lying beside him with our clothes tossed about, and the smell of dried sweat in the air, his entire being feels feral and sordid. Yet I can't bring myself to leave. I'm held spellbound by this coldness which emanates from him, carefully contained within an orchestrated civility. I'm convinced that I can break him down and remould him to be what I need. Women are built to believe we can restore men to their pure selves.

'Will you ever leave her?'

'No. She's a good sort. She's done nothing wrong.'

'And I have?'

'She doesn't deserve any of this. She doesn't know about you. At least you know why I can't be with you all the time.'

His code of honour is admirable except it asks nothing of him. There is no sacrificial pyre on which he will be required to burn the fat of his comfort. Even the occasional unsettling of his conscience can be blamed on the women in his life.

'Tell me about her,' I ask reluctantly, not really wanting to know.

He moves to the edge of the bed, furrowed and ridged by a worn duvet, and propping his head on his forearm, he tells me things about her, things I don't want to hear: the shape of her breasts, the curve of her butt, the noises she makes when she comes. I love kissing her breasts, he says, she has these beautiful breasts. He cups his hands, so I can get a measure of their size, and of their softness, I glean from the low moan that emits from his mouth. He tells me she'd come into his life through Kiran Mamaji's matchmaking. He'd flown to Bombay to meet this shy girl-woman, and married her at a posh club in Juhu, ten years ago. He tells me she works as a librarian at the Horton Library on the High Street. I realise our paths might have crossed, oblivious of a symmetry of purpose the universe sometimes slips into strangers' lives.

'Why don't you have kids?'

'It just didn't happen for us.'

'Do you love her?'

'She's a beautiful woman.'

'I hate you.'

'I know.'

We argue for what seems like hours, erratically pleading, swearing and making love, unable to sustain any one emotion for long. Spent and exhausted, I leave, late morning, not knowing if I'd ever see him again, not knowing if I'd ever tell him what I had intended to that night.

7

The Permanence of Place

The wooden footbridge I'm waiting on runs over a clayish canal, pallid and ebbed low. At the bottom of the bridge is the Horton Primary School which Sujata and I had attended. Her parents still live on the cul-de-sac not far from the school where all the houses look the same and the only distinguishing feature is the make of car parked outside. When we were young, Sujata's mother would sit by the street with other Gujarati and Sindhi neighbours and watch the kids play. They'd be eating *bhajas* whilst talking about life in East Africa. Someone would laughingly call themselves 'White Africans,' but they were neither white nor African. They were the children of empire, Indians from the former colonies of East Africa, who came here when Africa was decolonised in the 1960s; they were the in-between people, inhabiting a space between white colonial usurpation and black indigenous indignity. Brown is a colour defined by not being white or black and it takes on definitions depending on circumstance. We wear the colour of the oppressor and the oppressed, in solidarity with the dominant and the submissive, charming as chameleons and bargain-brokers. Sometimes, one of them would say, 'Why are we all here where the houses are so small and we don't have any servants?'

Someone else would reply, 'That's London, innit?'

They'd all groan in agreement that their life here was miserable, and how they'd had their own chickens and fruit trees in the back garden in Entebbe or Nairobi or Mombasa, and how they always had a shot-gun in the house because the lions could get really close. I listened to these stories whilst playing with Sujata. Horton seemed so many lands away from this magical place called Africa. Then one of them would ask, 'But would you return to Africa?' A sudden hush would descend on those gathered.

Sometimes a fast car would drive by dangerously close to the kerb, and crease the quiet of the street but otherwise nothing ever happened in Horton that was even remotely filled with intrigue.

A full moon blooms blue over the water. The familiar shape of Sujata is walking towards me in a haze of cigarette smoke. When she reaches me, I slip my hand in hers and squeeze it shut like a large heart. She inhales deeply of her cigarette, blows out and says, 'Wha'sup? Why all the mystery?'

'Those things will kill you.'

'Really? You think, they'll beat me to it?' She smiles.

The thing that we avoid talking about or divulging to anyone else, is that when Sujata was twenty-one, she tried to kill herself.

Sujata is walking fast and I'm finding it difficult to keep up with her just as when we were kids, always moving about, unable to keep still. A siren creak opens the gate to the green field. A milky fog floats amidst the trees. The earth reveals its squelch underfoot and I sink in its bog. I crouch like a flightless bird on the wet grass and pull Sujata down with me. The moon peers over the thicket, its craggy rock of blue exposed by the night.

'We haven't been here since primary school,' I say.

'I miss it too. I was afraid of childhood but I was even more afraid when childhood ended.'

'I saw Jassi yesterday.'

I don't mention the other time near Dr Yates' office or that she'd been jeering at me.

'Where?'

'On the bus.'

'What was that loser up to?'

'Going home after her shift, I guess.'

'I heard her husband left her for a white woman. He doesn't bother about the two kids either.'

'I didn't know she was married.'

'She got married soon after secondary school. She was barely eighteen.'

'Do you think she's just bitter now? I mean bitter toward everyone she knew at primary school.'

'She was a miserable loner at primary.'

'I was too, but I always had you.'

Sujata and I had known at once that we were kindred spirits. We were ghouls with hollowed-out eyes, staring at each other vacantly. We looked around at the other children, and even the ones that looked like us did not interest us. We were not like those smelling of home, those longing for home, those made raw by the sun, those wanting the sun on their backs, those with awkward smiles, those with their small steps sliding into runs. We sang the same nursery rhymes, practiced our phonics, observed the etiquette required of us, but we were not like them. We were conjoined twins sharing a lonely heart.

We realised early on that it was not the constancy

of people but the permanence of place, that would save us. So we discovered the green field with its brambled seclusion and bending trees backing onto the school. Within the faithfulness of place, familial failures could melt away, and specified rules could be observed to create an unshifting reality. It was in this seasonal space of uncut grass, turning leaves and slushes of snow, that some sense of the people we would become emerged for Sujata and me.

Later at university, we'd shared a flat between the three of us—Nathu (Sujata's lover at the time), Sujata and I—and that weekend when I was away, Nathu had found her lying limp on their bed. The ride to the hospital was riddled with pothole-induced vomiting. Sujata later claimed that the potholes saved her life. The reason why she tried to kill herself was not entirely clear; something about her father. Sujata seldom spoke of her father. Only, I noticed once, she flinched when he tried to touch her hair. By the time she was thirteen, she'd declared unceremoniously that she never wanted to have children. Why? I'd asked. Can't stand the slimy things, she'd said as if referring to tree frogs left on the lab table for dissection. Sujata and I had that in common: fathers who were a gaping void into which we stared, trying to make sense of ourselves.

Family and lover sprayed with guilt with her attempted suicide, there was enough residual guilt left over for me, my sense of failure never greater than in that moment, to assume lifelong custody of Sujata.

The moon strobes its pale blue light greying the grass at our ankles. Sujata lights another cigarette.

'I want to grant you lasting power of attorney, if anything happens to me,' I tell her.

'What's going to happen to you?'

'You never know.'

'Are you taking the piss?'

'No, I'm not. This is serious.'

'For fuck's sake, Anna-Marie, you're twenty-six years old. What is going to happen to you?'

'I don't know Sujata, but if something does happen to me, and I can't make decisions for myself, I want you to take care of things that need taking care of.'

Sujata turns to look me in the eye: 'I'm the one with problems, not you. Really, just tell what it is you think is going to happen to you?'

Out here on the field, the wind can turn without warning, and I feel it now whipping my face, brutal and unrelenting. I shiver involuntarily.

'Sujata, will you just agree to this one thing without all the questions?'

Our voices carry to the houses on the hem, their shrillness sliding through window sills. We've startled the sleepy sparrows roosting in the trees. They flap their flecked wings and squabble noisily. Sujata looks dejectedly at the clumpy mud on her shoes.

'I just worry about you. That's all,' she says, rocking back and forth wrapping her arms around herself.

'I know you do. But I need you to trust me right now.'

I can almost hear the chambers of Sujata's heart open and shut to let in the air she needs to clarify her thoughts—the thought that I might be dying. But really, I've never felt more alive in my life. Never felt more acutely the need to live.

8

Gliding on Wings

Snow crusts on wintry shrubs; it blinds wide-paned windows, it trickles in pearl-drop tears. Sanjay is gone. The things you miss lie in the absence of their occurrence: the anticipation of receiving a call, the door opening, the pulsing body, the warm breath, the febrile-fingered tongue, the illusion of a picket-fence future. The things you regret are the things that turn on their head: memory shrivelled to a footnote and possibility soured to a pickle.

With my heart bruised black, I ask Sanjay why he won't see me again.

'I have to look out for No. 1,' he says, 'which in my case is me.'

Sanjay was never *le grand amour*. He was just the hope of Him, baptized in water and crowned in thorns. The knot tightens and grows, and I am woman floundering, unravelling, not knowing what happens next. The uncertainty of the future is the real death, the real mourning, the real pain. If the future could be divined, then there would be no grief, no God, no need for hope to act as an intermediate balm, for life would cease to be a journey of encounters; it would simply be a point of arrival. I seek senselessly to divine a future, amidst this shapeless pain, in the arms of willing men.

I'm on my way to Hayes. On the red bus, sitting next to Mr Hashimi, the displaced Iranian asylum seeker, is

Mr Hussain, the long-suffering, racially bullied Pakistani, both of whom I know from the People's Advice Bureau where I work, and where they come in twice a month looking for free advice. Two old Punjabi ladies with trolley shopping bags block the aisle for a harried mum and her four runny-nosed kids. Clumps of mud are stuck to my seat, and a sneakered foot rests dangerously close to my face. With the smell of sweat and sick riding up my nose, and a press of people pushing to the back, the bus wends its way through Hayes High Street.

Places, like people, can be entirely self-important or utterly neglected. It's hard to imagine that a place like Hayes exists at all in London, where not a single ruddy English face can be found for streets on end, and the red in tooth and claw immigrant thrives under canopy-covered shops selling plastic buckets, fruit, fish, meat, jewellery, bedsheets, kaftans, salwars, headscarves, cakes, carrot halwa, samosas, carpets, curtains, and immigration advice to anyone who needs it. Here worlds collide in a babble of alien tongues but from a distance all languages sound alike; articulations of a desire to be heard and understood.

I often wonder if Mummy's Sylvia Plath would have committed suicide if she'd lived in Hayes. Perhaps some primal instinct would have compelled her to survive. Would Hayes have inspired her to write poetry or deadened her sense of the sublime? For there are two Londons really, one of self-fulfilling prophecy and the other of burnt-out dreams.

We were living in Hayes when Sujata tried to kill herself, in a pebbledash house on the intersection where the north road leads to the tennis club and a right-turn takes the driver to shops of irate South Indian fruit-sellers and blood-splattered Bangladeshi butchers. Back then, in 2011, we shared two rooms among the three of us—Nathu, Sujata and I—and the rusted pipes of a communal toilet with God knows how many others in the house. But this was all we could afford in our last year at university.

'In upstairs room, Polish girl shot by her boyfriend with crossbow,' the Indian landlord, Mr Channa, told us on our first day.

'With crossbow? What was he, a medieval archer?' Sujata laughed.

'Don't laugh, please. Poor girl bleeding right there on carpet. I had to call ambulance. I had to clean carpet.' He said this with a sense of annoyance rather than compassion.

I said, 'Right, anything else?'

'I don't want any trouble here. Okay? I don't want police here at night. All those troubles, I don't want. No drugs, no drinks. You stay clean. You stay out of trouble. You don't complain to no one about this place. You have problem, you come to me. You know what I mean?'

He picked his filthy teeth, watching us all the while, every movement in his body slowed by unhealthy corpulence.

'Okay,' we said.

It all felt so fashionably shabby, liberating and temporary, and it was only a twenty-minute drive to Horton, where our families still lived, mostly in fear that Hayes would one day spill into their quiet lives.

This I know for sure. The months before Sujata tried

to kill herself, we were doing ordinary things: checking emails, Googling, scraping the limescale from the kitchen taps, drinking wine out of a box, dancing to Amy Winehouse with our headsets on because the lascivious landlord, Mr Channa, who lived on the ground floor, and felt for the crack of our butt at every opportunity, didn't like music. This I'm not sure of: that I encouraged Nathu.

It was the end of summer, the whiskered grass dying, the yellowed leaves scattering with scant regard on asphalt roads. I was bored and restless and vague about my future. I was swimming in a fish-bowl, making splashing sounds, wanting to jump out and join a braver world because I'd outgrown my little make-believe universe populated by Mummy, Sujata, university professors, the dusty potted plants in my room, and the Indian sari curtains on its windows. I could see the glass bowl reflecting me, deflecting from a world-view trimmed and narrow. I sensed, without knowing, a world beyond me. I swore in my saner moments that I'd never want things larger than me or a life that would exclude Sujata. But I have often found it difficult to survive long periods of self-imposed sanity and my sanity's shifting tectonic plates are particularly vulnerable to boredom and insecurity.

I'd like to think Nathu could have been more responsible in that room with its peeling paint and greasy floors when he appeared wearing just his boxer shorts. I'd like to think he could have pulled back because he was the one in a committed relationship, not me, he was the brilliant one reading law at university, but he was young and silly, just like me, and there was something bestial about our desire. We lived above morality and common sense. The constraints of society did not apply to us. We were incapable of understanding time, and that on a time continuum, human decency is essential for civilisation—for love, for friendship to survive. But we existed entirely in the moment, a flickering flame, a conquistador's triumph.

Nathu's shadow shoaled across my bedroom walls, the morning we'd run out of hot water. Sujata had gone to her mother's house to shower. He said he wanted to talk.

'About Sujata?'

'She's been acting strange.'

'Really? I hadn't noticed.'

'She worries all the time. She paces. She rocks. She screams in her sleep.'

'She's always been a worrier. Even when we were at school, she worried endlessly. But I'd know if something was really wrong.'

He shrugged and sat on the edge of the bed. Last night's beer had flooded my bladder, I was feeling fragile and full; I needed to pee but I sat beside him instead. I could feel his body radiating a raw heat. I could smell his buttery-breath. I hated buttery-breath. It reminded me of dodgy drunk uncles in oversized coats, trying to cop a feel at Goan community dances. But I moved closer to him, to feel his breath plume on my skin. There is always a singular moment of clarity before an act of madness but I've learned to override the impulse to shift gears to neutral. Instead, I ramp up wanting to know what it feels like at the edge of the cliff, that sick feeling of exhilaration when death is imminent and yet you believe completely, as only the young do, in your ability to survive and conquer mortality. In my twisted mind, I imagined laughing with Sujata about Nathu's buttery-breath. I wanted to prove once and for all that I was as desirable as Sujata with her perfect oval face, her long silky hair and her thin body. How beautiful she looked that year; men came up to her and asked if she was a model, or if she wanted to become one. They said they could get her a job in television or with the airlines, jobs that need women to look beautiful without feeling guilty about looking beautiful. Her mere existence gave men pleasure, the sort of visceral jolt and vertiginous joy which left them senseless, trembling and pleading. Sujata had that effect on people, the sort I never had. Even little children gazed at her with their big, liquid eyes, wanting to be cared for by her.

She'd laugh and say, 'Not interested, mate.'

I was desperately jealous. Not in the way harsh, vulgar girls are jealous of those more accomplished and better-looking than them, but in the way siblings are jealous of not getting the lion's share of attention, and then subtly planning ways to thwart their rival sibling's success.

Nathu had stopped talking.

'Would you like me to undress?' I asked.

I knelt on the bed and peeled off my T-shirt to reveal two large breasts with hardened nipples. I shivered slightly, partly because it was cold, but more so because I was afraid he'd ask me to put my clothes back on. The room shrunk to a crypt, light leaked out of it, the air turned dense, only my pounding heart told me that I was still alive. I was awaiting a burial under a mound of shame. But he leaned into my face, his eyes lowered, his breathing ragged, an erection visibly straining against his shorts.

'I'm not good at this,' he whispered, his body taut and self-conscious.

'Neither am I,' I said, kissing his bobbing Adam's apple. The room became an echo chamber of laboured breathing.

'This idea that people have to be good at this is ridiculous,' I added, falling back on the bed.

He sat facing me, watching me intently: 'Maybe experienced is the more accurate word then.'

'Are you always so precise just before shagging?'

We laughed. His mouth covered mine in an awkward push, the lips loose and longing. Then the rest of him was upon my unresisting body.

Later, we stood by the window, naked, content, unmindful of the passing world, cushioned safely inside a sanctuary of swollen pride, and we drew dreams on dusty panes, maps of the magnificent futures awaiting us.

Nathu glanced at the loose pile of books lying on the window ledge; too distracted to inspect them closely, he asked me, 'What are you reading?'

'Junot Diaz.'

'The Latino writer?'

'Yes, he writes about *tias* and *tios*, aunties and uncles. As a Goan, I can relate to Latin culture.'

'That's strange, to relate to something so foreign.'

'I'm strange and complicated.' I looked up at him, smiling. He pulled away from the window, placed his hands on my face and kissed me. His hands were delicate, his eyes were brightly lit, his mouth a fleshy petal. I shivered, this time with mounting desire, thinking of his long-limbed body pressed against me. Sujata's face, sombre and uncomprehending, bobbed briefly before me, but I pushed it away.

'I like complicated,' he said, moaning softly.

We spoke about E.M. Forster and George Orwell because second-generation immigrant Goans and Bengalis do not share Indian poets or philosophers in common except those that belong to the empire. We borrow everything from Britain and we grow up thinking it belongs to us, sculpting our inner selves. But I believed then that Nathu and I belonged to something larger, something rooted deeper, which spoke an ancient language, calling us to journey to our hidden selves, an unspoken binding that was greater than the nation we knew.

Pointing to the street, Nathu said, 'Did you know London used to be a walled settlement?'

'Really?'

'Yes, the Romans built a defence wall around it.'

'And here we are in the twenty-first century, still putting up walls even if we can't see them.'

'Look at all those people down there. Escaping their own countries: migrants, refugees; nameless, faceless people with their pasts erased and futures unknown. It's so easy to erase oneself.'

He stood behind me now, his crotch pressing into my back, his hands, clumsy but comforting, tracing the curve of my spine. I tried to think about what he was saying, but my mind was muddled, and kept wishing for his fingers to find the places that yearned for them.

'Citizens of the world. That's what I call them,' I said hoarsely, barely able to breathe. He continued talking, whilst pressing harder against me.

'You believe in open borders, then?'

'No nation should refuse entry to those who need it.'

'Anna-Marie, let's not pretend we have the answers,' he said slowly, as if explaining it to a child, 'especially not us students with our campus politics.'

His webbed fingers sought the underside of my bottom. A moan caught in my mouth. I was afraid someone from the street would look up, and see my open-mouthed face pressed against the pane.

'What do you mean?'

'Are you willing to listen? Truly listen to an opposing viewpoint?'

He said this despite my quivering body wanting release, but he toyed with me. Why did he do it? Because…it had been important to his young self to assert his supremacy, to regain control the only way he knew how, by declaring victory over my body, over me. His hands fumbled and betrayed his inexperience, but he was bold and self-assured, without apology or hesitation, about his place in the world.

'I try,' I said, weakly.

'Then I put it to you, that we don't have the answers to everything. We are fumbling, fumbling, fumbling about in the dark. Fumbling without experience. Our righteous rage, our desire to exist on spectrums—left-wing, right-wing—is just hysterical panic. As if life is that simple, as if life has ever been that simple, as if life is ever going to be that simple.'

I turned and looked pleadingly: he drew me into his body. With a few sucking breaths, our bodies juddered and slackened against each other. He caught me then, folding me into the wingspan of his arms. I kissed him, abruptly, gratefully, and clasped his hands in solidarity.

'We are fumbling without compassion and empathy,' I said.

Outside unveiled a sky darkening with cloud. We opened the window and stretched our arms out to the world. Those first few droplets of rain, melancholy and wet, dribbled on our skin still unblemished by life. We laughed like Icarus, gliding on wings. The deluge that came later, we wouldn't survive.

The bus hisses to a stop at Hayes Tesco, where I get off. My Aunt Cielo has set me up on a blind date. I'm meeting him at a Hayes South Indian restaurant right next door to a fishmonger. The smell of raw fish carries through the dining hall on a wet wind. All around, people speak in Tamil and women in silk saris rustle past me smelling of sandalwood soap.

The man appears in a green suit, a small garden gnome come to life. We sit at a table; he spreads his hands over the large menu, and suggests a special dosa I should order. A clean-shaven waiter arrives, notepad in hand and takes our order. After the waiter retreats, the conversation skims over disparate stories in our lives:

'What do you do?'

'Is that what you dreamed of doing?'

'Do you imagine doing that all your life?'

'What is it women really want, nowadays?'

'Are men looking to commit to women or just take them out on dates?'

'What do you think of blended families?'

All the while we try to guess where the other person stands on the issues, at times expressing faux exasperation at our life's choices, as if by doing so we are opening ourselves to each other, laying ourselves bare, taking responsibility for our bad decisions and vowing to make better ones in the future. None of this is true, of course.

Our fingers meet accidentally across the table. That feels like a violation of my body. I imagine what it might be like to go home with this Green-man sitting with me in the fish-smelling restaurant, what it might feel like to let Green-man undress me, his froglike legs upon me, his grasshopper arms around me, his reptilian tongue in me. The thought repulses me. Everything about Green-man repulses me. Despite their best selves, Green-men are destined to remain irrelevant to me. Because what my body needs, and what my twisted soul needs is something else entirely. I have to believe that the algorithm of fate will deliver it to me.

9

The Drawbridge Pulled Up

It's May, crocuses preen in parks, the cats are in the hedgerow, the morning has emptied into a clear blue sky. This is the circus of birth, death and renewal. In between is the high-wire trapeze act called life, intensified through pain or happiness. Mother once told me that Sylvia Plath worried constantly about growing old and dying without being 'Somebody'. I worry about growing old and dying without ever really knowing 'Somebody'. But with each passing year, I've come to realise that knowing someone is a fantasy. Most people though, at least, bear the wisdom of their own carefully curated history and offer it glibly at a moment's notice to strangers. But not me. For me, the past and the present are disparate parts. Fathers, the custodians of lineage, are supposed to be that link which makes life a linear progression. But Daddy is absent to me.

Abdu arrives at nine sharp.

'You can't park the bike inside the office,' I say.

'Why not? It's not bothering anyone.'

The people waiting in the reception area at the People's Advice Bureau turn to watch as Abdu takes his bike out and locks it to a pipe running the length of the building.

'It's not safe outside,' Abdu says, as he takes his seat beside me and plops a coffee thermos on the desk.

'This isn't Nigeria. No one is going to steal your bike.'

'Nigerians don't steal. They're quality people.'

There's a titter from the people crowding reception. Abdu has made London's underclass feel better about themselves. Whatever else happens, at least they're not in Nigeria. Suddenly, I belong to those people, to that titter which I've caused, and which the world over smugly drains into pools of prejudice against immigrants.

At ten in the morning, a lengthening shadow looms at the office door. I recognise him instantly. When his number's called, he pulls a chair at my desk and sinks heavily into it; his face swollen with drink. Already I want to escape, hide behind the box-files, make my excuses and hand him over to Abdu, who is busy dispensing food vouchers to a Syrian woman. Working at the People's Advice Bureau, I'm anaesthetised to life's injustices: poverty, displacement, discrimination, all shrivel like seeds into something small, to be filed away in a cabinet at the end of the day. The last thing I want is a file name with a past of which I'm intimately aware and which I might just care about.

He looks at me, his eyes narrowing, searching for clues to explain the jolt of familiarity. He's turned out exactly as I imagined he would. Tall, thin, a few faint lines already forming about the taut lips, the teeth yellowed, the hands calloused. A smock of thoughts gather in my mind. Did he end up with Annie? Does he have kids? Why is he in Hayes? Does he remember that afternoon in his bedroom?

'Hello, Daniel. What brings you in here?'

He lights up in recognition.

'Well, I'll be damned. If it ain't bumbling Anna-Marie. Right proper grown up, yeah?'

'How can I help you?'

'Straight to it then? I'm going to be evicted, innit?'

'Renting in Hayes?'

He nods.

'With your family?'

'With Shirley and them two kids. That shitface landlord says he can't do anything about it.'

'Have you been paying your rent?'

'Done my back in, haven't I? Out of a job, innit?'

'On Job Seekers Allowance?'

'Yes.'

'And you're overdue by how many months?'

'About two months.'

'Utilities and phone?'

'Haven't paid them either.'

'Have you received an eviction notice?'

'Nah, he ain't going to bother to do this proper like. Just wants us gone. He's going to change the locks on us for sure. Like we was trash.'

'Actively looking for a job, are you?'

'Doing my best, ain't I? Not like jobs are lined up for a good-looking fella like me.'

He winks at me then. Some of his youthful cockiness emerges through the dense fog of destitution. His life is a fragile thing, dangling precariously between my help and homelessness. I don't voice my thoughts, I don't feel a loss of power holding them back; Daniel is already defeated.

'We're going to have to draw up a payment plan for you to manage your money.'

'Game on. I'm ready.'

'Would you be able to meet with Abdu here, on Wednesday?

'Yeah, absolutely. I've maximum respect for you lot.'

'Meanwhile, lie low. Don't open the door to anyone who claims to be a bailiff. You have rights.'

Some part of me wants to be rid of him as quickly as possible. Another part wants to stand on this link-bridge with Daddy for as long as I can.

Sensing this, Daniel asks, 'Why didn't you ever come back? It wasn't all on me, was it?'

'Daddy didn't exactly come looking for me either.'

'He were busy. He had a new baby on the way.'

'I wasn't part of Daddy's new family.'

'Why didn't you say something? You were very quiet back then.'

Daddy should have known: they must have meant something, all those unspoken words I gathered parsimoniously on my tongue, unspent in joy or sorrow, hoarded over time for the right moment to arrive. But I existed on the periphery of Daddy's consciousness, a blurry dot never merging with the main, the gates closed, the drawbridge pulled up.

'Little tot's grown up now. About to finish primary. Your old man's going to make sure he stays in school. Not like me. I dropped out, innit? Got my old room, the little blighter, Thomas.' He winks at me again crudely, sharing what he thinks is an inside joke. Daniel can't resist the overpowering male desire for conquest whatever the circumstance.

I start to clear the papers on my desk, signalling the end of the interview.

'Can you come at four on Wednesday?'

'Got nothing better to do, have I? You should go around the old place. Especially now.'

His eyes scan my bulging belly. The knot kicks benignly from its underwater world.

'How far gone are you?'

'Six months.'

For a moment, I'm back in his bedroom in that ugly house waiting for my life to begin. And now it has begun without anyone by my side.

Daddy has named his son Thomas after my grandfather. A brother I've never met can lay claim to Thomas More, Shakespeare and Winston Churchill, but also to me, tied to generations buried in untended graves far away. I feel that primal tug of longing for my family.

Daniel pushes back his chair and gets up.

'Righty-ho, I'm off. Go round and see the old man. Get in there, yeah? You and me, we was the same back then but I made my peace with them,' he says. I watch as he balls his fist, and walks out the door, thinning into the squabble of the street, the siren wail, the scabby buildings, the angry wastelands of broken Britain who make their peace with living on the margins.

10

Heliocentricity

In the autumn of receding suns and wind-dusted leaves, of university protests, gas pipe leaks, broken down trains and weekend engineering roadworks, like spritely ten-year-olds in tree houses, Nathu and I established the Horton Hideaway, where his dark body yielded so easily to my untutored touches, and his mouth opened in full-circles of gratitude just before he came. I loved the way light bladed his bare back as he collapsed on top of me, the slightly oiled locks of hair that tumbled onto his forehead, the traditional thread that diagonally cut across his chest scraping my skin. I imagined him having been a great Hindu warrior in a previous birth even though Catholicism had only ever acquainted me with martyred saints and avenging angels. There in the bedroom of my childhood discontent, we drank beer and ate Jammie Dodgers. Sometimes I'd sit up on rockpools of pillows, hugging my knees, watching him dust biscuit crumbs off his hairy chest, quoting Engels and Dilbert in the same breath. He rattled off Tagore from memory. I initiated him with the libidinous complexities of F.N. Souza's life. Unlike Sujata and I, Nathu didn't carry scars from life lessons. His brilliant mind was forged on the anvil of scholarly reading totally lacking in the sort of introspection lived experience brings, unburdened by the petty rituals of morality or codes of friendships formed in childhood when worlds are coloured by crayons.

'You're so naïve,' he'd say.

'About what?'

'About life, about everything. You want to fix the world.'

'You're an idiot, I don't want to fix it, I want to change it. You stand for the status quo and complacency.'

We delighted in our radical selves, him confessing to having joined the Conservative party membership, and me having a fondness for irredeemably flawed characters in books.

'Shush, don't tell anyone you're a Conservative. Conservatives don't get laid.'

'I'm getting laid right now.'

'You're a Tory Wonder Boy, aren't you?

'Tory Glory for this token darkie,' he roared, beating his chest. We laughed, and he buried his face in the hollow of my breasts, moaning deeply.

'Mother's turned into an activist,' I said to Nathu.

We were sitting in a near-empty restaurant in the City, with track lights trailing across the ceiling and leather-upholstered booths lined against the walls. I ran my fingers over the leather. It felt slippery and still smelt of cowhide. Nathu ordered a beer. Just one, he said apologetically, because really we couldn't afford the restaurant, and had only popped in to use the loo. I ordered a Coke. We dug into our pockets and pulled out whatever we had in loose change, to pay.

'What's she done now?' he asked, drinking half his beer in a gulp.

'She's joined a Horton community group who want to ban fireworks. Friends United Against Fireworks, it's called.'

As Diwali drew near, curtains of flickering lights had appeared on windows, elliptical *rangoli* flowered outside Horton homes, and for days, crackers had exploded like leaky green stars in the night sky.

'The FUAF? That's epic, man. What's her problem with fireworks?' he asked, licking his lips.

'They thicken the air with smoke and scare pets, she says.'

He turned toward me, letting his hand drop under the table, then sliding it swiftly between my legs and sinking his fingers deep into my flesh. I muffled a quickening moan into a paper napkin and stared out the window at the deserted car park. It was four in the afternoon; the world was on pause until five when the office crowd would submerge the streets. He brought his hand back up and laughed. His elongated fingers rested on the wooden tabletop and the lamplight above shone on them. I thought about how much pleasure he could give me, just by being the owner of his fingers, his tongue, his legs, and I felt fresh waves of desire rise within me, making me feel weak and miserable in some way, for I thought almost immediately of the pain he could exert by withholding those things from me. He could command my body at will and I would respond, a pilgrim to his calling. Where the light leaned on Nathu, his face seemed cruel, not because of anything he'd done but because of this emptiness he suddenly filled me with, and because he continued as before, oblivious to it.

'And they're a fire hazard. I'm with her on this. If firing crackers for a week was a British tradition, it'd be banned years ago. I hate minority appeasement,' he said after a while.

'But there's only Mr Singh on her street, and I'm not even sure he lights crackers. No, I know her. It's just her way of protesting anything connected with India.'

Nathu laughed, choking a little on his spittle. Then he drew me close to him and smiled: 'You don't hate me, do you?'

'Outside of India, Indians don't have the luxury of hating each other.'

'Even if we don't have anything in common? Come on, you know as well as I do, the Punjabis in Southall have nothing to do with the South Indians in East Ham.'

'Nothing like a common enemy to bring people together.'

'You mean the motherland of the colonial empire who we love to hate but want to migrate to?'

He was shaking his head when he said this, his lips curling in condescension. We argued. We laughed. I watched Nathu and realised he was filled with good cheer and I felt a light-hearted joy lifting me up. We called the waiter standing at the far end, glaring at us with growing disapproval. We ordered two fat juicy tuna steaks with mashed potatoes, and beans and carrots on the side, none of which I could afford. We ate with the eagerness of the young, paring our fish, smacking our lips and wiping our mouths. Nathu pulled out a credit card and placed it on the table. It was his father's, to be used only in emergencies, he explained.

'I don't have any money. I'll pay you back,' I promised. 'I just won't eat for the rest of the week.'

'You don't have to pay me, really, it's fine. I'll sort it out with Dad,' he assured me in a low voice. In his fierce kindness, I felt a deep sense of gratitude, and the beginning of something new. All around us, the booths filled up steadily with people in expensive suits and smart looks, people who had exciting jobs in the City, who spoke about middle-management, board meetings and staff training. Their voices rose and became a distinct body of noise, assailing the room with its authority. We felt jubilant as the evening wore on, and we longed to be part of this adult world, glistening with power.

Sujata and I stood by the window watching Khan's Driving School car pull out onto the road. The learner driver turned into the wrong lane.

'Will she be killed?' Sujata asked.

'No, of course not. Mr Khan will sort it.'

The car veered erratically towards a large man dispersing dead leaves with his leaf blower; the leaves lifted in a circular motion and scattered wildly but then just as swiftly settled down again. The street stood still as Mr Khan steadied the wheel and manoeuvred a three-point turn. Then the street breathed a sigh of relief and hurried back into motion.

'Do you think he's disturbed the bees?' she asked.

'Probably.'

'Will they come in here? Do you think they'll come in here? Anna-Marie, will they come in here?'

'Calm down. Even if they do, we'll just swat them away.'

'We can't open the window. We can't ever open the window, ever again.'

'This is crazy, Sujata. Close the window, then.'

She bolted the window shut and pulled the curtain across, abruptly darkening the room, lengthening the shadows within.

As autumn deepened, dreary and damp, a kind of unpredictability clung to Sujata, her eyes vivid with excitement or dulled with dissipation. She worried constantly about calamitous world events even though there wasn't the slightest chance that she'd be impacted by any of them; she obsessed about death and what came after death; she grew afraid to go to sleep because she was convinced she'd never wake up. She checked Google constantly. She drank wine a lot. I tried to be understanding, but the thing with fragile people is that their fragility is hardest on them, not on those tolerating it or countering it with logic and the mundane needs of day to day living.

'I can't live like this anymore,' she said, one day.

'We all feel that way sometimes,' I replied mechanically, and handed her a bag of Walker's crisps. 'These always cheer you up.'

As the skies folded into early nightfall, mothers shuttered their children indoors, rain seeped through our skin, and the last of Halloween's hollowed-out pumpkins were heaved into skips, a flat-footed silence, clumsy and cruel, crept into our lives and stayed there.

The week leading up to Remembrance Sunday in November, Mummy's living room turned into a floral tribute of red paper poppies stuck into window frames. John McCrae's poem 'In Flanders Fields' had been printed on paper and sellotaped to the wall.

'Why?' I asked.

'To honour the dead.'

'But Britain's wars had nothing to do with Goa.'

'That's the problem with the young. You don't know

your history. Hundreds of Goans working on British naval ships died during the war. I'd like to honour them, if you don't mind.'

'But I do mind, Mummy. The poppy doesn't commemorate other people's dead. Just our own. It's selfish and exclusionary.'

'You exasperate me. You have no respect for the past, for tradition, for family, for everything that came before you. You think only of yourself, living in the now.'

'The poppy is a racist symbol and it glorifies war.'

'Racist this and racist that. When you sign up to serve a country—any country—and are willing to die for it, I'll have some respect for your opinion. Really Anna-Marie, you're becoming one of those people who know the price of everything and the value of nothing. You don't value the sacrifices people have made so that your generation can enjoy the freedom that you do. Your father and you don't understand the importance of duty.' She said this just before closing the door, red poppy firmly pinned to blue cardigan, and carry-case in hand. I realised she'd veered off the topic of duty to the nation and was pontificating on how Daddy and I should have been duty-bound to her. Aunt Cielo and she were spending the weekend in Mitcham where the Goan Chaplaincy was conducting a memorial service.

Nathu and I spent the weekend together at Mummy's house, grateful for Mummy's emotive respect for the war dead. We moved in with packs of beer, a bucket of fried chicken, and two pizzas. At mid-day, someone parked outside the gate. We scampered out of bed. We waited silently for the key to turn in the lock. Any moment now, Mummy would walk through the door and find us naked. Then we heard the clang of metal and the rustle of paper. It was just the Royal Mail postman pushing letters through the mail slot. We jumped back into bed, relieved, and set upon each other like dogs.

We stayed up late watching reruns of *Goodness Gracious Me*, trying to speak like the Kapoors.

'I quite understand why the Kapoors wanted to be the Coopers,' Nathu said, tucking a pizza box into the folds of our blanket. The room smelt of something feral, like a pen that had not been cleaned out for days.

'You mean slowly become English? Do we have to? Can't we just be ourselves living in England?'

'What does being yourself mean? You're surrounded by a dominant culture. You're bound to be subsumed by it. A dominant culture is dominant for a reason. It's aspirational. My parents see it as a path to success. Anyway, identity politics bores me to death.'

'But these things matter, don't they? To feel a sense of belonging within your own community, to identify with your race and the unique experience of that race.'

'Your experience of being Asian is not the same as mine. I don't know what it means to be Goan. And what do you know about being a Bengali? We can't have experienced Britain in the same way.'

'What do you mean?'

'You being Catholic made it possible for you to go to a great Catholic secondary school. I being middle-class made it possible for me to shop at Waitrose. You must at least be able to claim the uniqueness of your own experience. Anyway, race doesn't matter to me. I'm British, born of London, and I can make my own way in life without playing the race card, thank you very much.'

I thought about that for a while and felt confused

by what Nathu was saying. Was he not part of us, those milling on the margins who had to fight just to exist? So little remained of ourselves if we emptied it of community. Did Nathu not feel the same way? But I was lying next to him, our bodies touching, and I didn't feel marginal just then.

'You know, I could do this forever,' he said, leaning towards me.

'What? Eat pizza in bed and argue with me?'

'No, I mean be with you. Like this, just the two of us.'

A shower of leaves rained from the oak tree by the window. Something shifted imperceptibly, altering my sense of what lay ahead. I had by instinct, circumnavigated my way to love, peeling away layers to reach it, and now I was on the high seas, on a rite of passage into the unknown. I felt the sweep of trade winds, the currents of rising rivers. He had uttered the word forever, a word so profound, its meaning was wrapped up in time and space, and the tunnels that connect them both. Sujata still didn't know about us. He was still with Sujata, but swore they were not intimate. I had assumed whatever was happening between us would stop at some point. But now I felt the stirring of something transcendent—a oneness with his essential self. I wanted to archive these emotions for I sensed I would draw on them in later life to sustain me. I pressed myself into his body, scared and vulnerable, yet strong and ready for a future together. Out there, in the vastness of the night was a thump and a thud, a rattle and a rustle. For the first time since Daddy left, I felt safe.

Mummy was full of stories about the wholesome Father Xavier, on her return, Monday morning. She entered my room and stood still, shocked at the disarray: bedcovers crumpled, books tossed about and pizza crumbs in trails. I sprung out of bed and threw my arms around her, steeped in happiness as I was. She rolled her eyes and assumed I was going through another 'finding myself' phase. And I was, really. Never had the face of self-discovery been so intense, poignant and beautiful. Like all only children, Nathu and I believed completely in the heliocentricity of our existence. Everyone else blurred from our line of vision.

11

Dreams Fragile Like Eggs

Mummy still rents the house Daddy and she had lived in, before I was born, before the world became an intricate web of three lives. Even after Daddy left, and she had managed to get a decent enough job at the *Horton People* magazine, she refused to leave. But the neighbourhood has changed. Condemned houses bear the burden of the prolonged recession, while open patches of grassland where once children played, have iron pillars birthing new buildings as part of the Horton urban renewal project. Most of the old families, those who knew each other, have dispersed like pollen to germinate elsewhere. The post-office where Daddy once worked has closed down, family-owned stores are stripped bare and boarded up, the old pubs have morphed into supermarkets owned by faceless conglomerates. Beyond Horton's dead chimneys, its breath of stippling spores and salty sea, is concrete creeping in.

The walk through Horton High Street takes me past Bollywood Style Salon with its smell of peroxide heavy on the windless strip. I'm tempted to go in, to ask for a full body wax, so that when I'm fully naked and at my most vulnerable, Jassie might feel inclined to explain why she had laughed at me outside of Mattie's, and shown me the middle-finger on the bus. I peer through the window and see a large woman stretched out in a reclining chair, as if on a rack, her head tilted back, her legs extended out. Jassie's face hovers over hers, an almost invisible silken thread held between her mouth and fingers expertly shears the woman's facial hair. Jassie seems utterly sadistic in that fluorescent-lit moment, enjoying the pain she is inflicting as she works her fingers frantically like a puppeteer. I unspool the reel of memories I hold of Jassie, and I can't find a single one of significance. An occasional waxing cannot count as significant enough to encourage jeering. And yet, I must have touched Jassie's life in an untoward way for her pain to fester and erupt as it does when I meet her. Had I, in some imperceptible manner, told Jassie that I found her studded tops, fake nails and sweaty leggings repulsive? Or that her constant gabbing in Punjabi on the mobile was just rude and never done in polite company. Or that vocational training was not the same as university. Had a raised eyebrow, a pursed lip, a blank stare at the laundromat or the local co-op, the tell-tale signs of my self-righteous indignation, become obvious to her?

Jassie's breasts are now pressed hard against the woman's head and her mouth has acquired a certain rhythm with the silken thread. My own need to know about Jassie's injured ego feels indulgent and petty in the midst of this precarious act, so I carry on down the street.

When I reach Hollyfield Road, Mummy's neighbour, Mr Skinner, is unloading a truck in their garden. Bags of black soil slide heavily onto the flat earth. His two sons are pushing wheelbarrows filled with potted plants to the front end of the garden. It feels like a lot of trouble in a neighbourhood which has filled their gardens with gravel.

'Morning, beautiful day,' Mr Skinner says to me, doffing his hat.

'Glorious day for a spot of gardening. Have you heard about the sighting in the Thames?' I ask.

'Mark my words, it's just some wreckage jutting out,' he replies.

'Let's hope it's a monster from the lochs.'

'What's happened to your young fella that used to come round? Is he the father?' he asks, pointing to my belly.

I avoid his gaze; he must have spotted Nathu back then. We're distracted by his daughter in a pink dress, crying in a corner of the garden for no apparent reason. Mrs Skinner comes out, scoops her up and kisses her face. Palely, the girl falls silent, needing no balm other than that of touch. I stand mummified, transfixed by this glimpse into the esoteric mysteries of motherhood.

'See you la'er,' I say, opening the wrought-iron gate to Mummy's inadequate garden of loose gravel and withering shrubs. The front door is ajar. I push it open and call out to Mummy.

'I'm in the kitchen, stranger. No one remembers me. Maybe I should be dead. That's the only way Goans are remembered. In obituaries.'

'You're fifty-six, Mummy. Goans don't die at fifty-six, anymore. Advances in medical science have been made. The National Health Service is quite remarkable.'

The kitchen smells of coriander leaves and green chillies; the rising crescendo of clanging pots means Mummy is nearing the end of her thinning patience.

She's washing rice in a colander. I know the process. Wash. Drain. Drop in a pot of boiling water. Within minutes, puffs of cooked white rice will emerge ready for the serving.

'The kitchen is where your grandmother cluttered my life with her dreams,' Mummy says, 'they were small and fragile like eggs, watery like milk. A working-class grocery list, that's what her dreams were. When I grew up I decluttered.'

'She was a real Hitler,' Cielo says, emerging from the pantry. Cielo, like most Goans, has a strange fascination with European dictators, naming her two sons Franco and Salazar.

'Hello, Aunty.' I kiss her talcum-powdered face fumy with Sarson's vinegar and English lavender.

'You're glowing,' she says, waving me away but pleased with the affection. 'Pregnancy suits you. Too bad there's no father on the scene.' Cielo has the curious ability to compliment and condemn in the same breath. The world feels unsafe from these two moon-faced, topsy-turvy women whose shifting ground slides into constant paradox and uncertainty.

Mummy takes a Princess Diana tea-towel—always a royalist—and wipes the sweat pearling on her brow. 'Menopause is rough on a woman. You watch out for it. Before you know it, your ovaries will be husks. One minute a Madonna and the next a toothless hag.' She pulls a face, pointing a wooden ladle at my protruding belly.

I observe with a tinge of childish fear (the primal part of me that never wants Mummy to age), the clumps of sweat circling her arms, the straggly streaks of grey on her head, the spread of fat on her hips. She is a celestial star fading into dry barrenness, her once-wet dreams thinning into shadows, their ferocity folding in the gloaming. She who had fought so hard to break away from the old, also forgot how to grow old without feeling a sense of failure. She misses Daddy.

'You don't really believe women become worthless as they age, do you?'

'Of course, they do,' the two women chorus in unison.

'Look at Grandma Anna's life. Look at my life. I'm invisible to the world,' Mummy says.

'You never say anything nice about Grandma Anna.'

'That's because she was not a nice woman. She spent her entire life in the kitchen. You remember, Cielo, how uncomfortable she felt if father asked her to come out of the kitchen?'

Cielo nods in acknowledgment: 'She expected us girls to wake up at four in the morning and tend to the paddy fields. She had no ambition for her daughters' futures. Her sons were everything to her.'

I turn to Mummy, incredulous at this revelation. 'You worked the paddy fields, Mummy?'

'In Goa. We all did. All three of us girls.'

'How did you manage school, then?'

'Your Grandpa was an incredible man. He insisted I stay on and study. He bought me a bicycle to ride to school. Was it mother's jewellery he pawned to buy the bike, Cielo?'

Cielo looks up from cutting onion and wipes the tears from her eyes with the embroidered handkerchief she always keeps tucked in her cleavage. Some of her talcum powder smears the handkerchief. There's an exaggerated clearing of the throat: 'She was so angry with your Mummy,' she says, 'didn't speak to her for a month. She could be cruel like that. Refusing to look at us if she was angry. Refusing to eat until we showed remorse. Once, she even threatened us with a knife. We were so afraid of her moody outbursts, no?'

I sit on a kitchen stool, my elbows on the counter, listening to my mother and my aunt talk. There's an observable tenderness between them wrung from that terrifying instance when siblings first discover their mother could be a monster, and know this to be a rejection of them. That knowledge, shameful and frightening to a child whose very existence depends on the judicious goodwill of parents, becomes bearable only because they have each other.

The steam from the rice turns the kitchen into a muggy swamp. Mummy stands by the stove, bravely withstanding the heat, waiting for the rice to come to boil. She says, 'Father sold a small property he owned and sent me to St Xavier's in Bombay. That Gothic quadrangle with its flourishes and fleurons was where I came alive. Poetry and philosophy flowed through leather-bound books and into me.'

'But you hate Bombay, why did you stay?'

'Because my father died. How old were you, Cielo, when father died?'

'Oh, I was very young. About sixteen, I think. And there were two more mouths to feed after me.'

'Father died of a massive heart-attack. Just another man who deserted me. I was the eldest. I had to find a job. There were plenty of jobs in Bombay.' She sighs, deeply.

Steadily, I become aware of how difficult life had been for Mummy and the choices forced upon her by the vagaries of fate. But Mummy had never viewed circumstance as anything other than opportunity.

The starchy rice liquid bubbles over. Eyes squinting, jaw clenched, Mummy holds down the pot in the sink and drains the water; she heaps the rice onto three white plates and ladles cubed, curried pork on top. Cielo adds cucumbers and tomatoes drizzled in vinegar to the offering. Then she twists the top off a bottle of white wine and pours two glasses. Cielo and Mummy have remained faithful to Goa in so many ways. They still walk to Jeanie's Master Bakers for spongy bread, which reminds them of home. London has not essentially changed the two women and I wonder if it is at all possible to change in later life or if our paths are determined early on, and then we're locked in, rewinding the same play over and over again, incapable of discovering new ideas, resigned to a preordained destiny of sorts. The sisters are a gale force wind as siblings often are, and I feel outnumbered by them.

Mummy stands in the centre of the kitchen with plates of rice in either hand. Let's take our lunch in there, she says, pointing down the hallway. I follow her through the door. A harsh light pours into the living room, the afternoon sun is fierce and casts long shadows on the plasterboard walls painted long years ago. Memories meld into the faded curtains and balding carpet. I remember when small joys had blushed like buttercups here. Mummy and Daddy jiving to Elvis Presley songs, whilst London beamed through the windows. But then memories are like mirages on isolated roads—untrustworthy.

'What made you come to London?' I ask, sitting on a shapeless bean bag, forking soggy rice into my mouth.

'When your father and I became Portuguese citizens, I thought of emigrating. You know, Portugal still allows Goans to become citizens, right? Daddy didn't want to leave the comforts of middle-class Bombay. All those dances at the gymkhana and all that. But I did.'

'You must have loved him, once.'

Mummy looks at Cielo and blushes like a young bride in her bridal chamber. Mummy doesn't answer but Cielo does: 'A real rogue, he was. Made decent money as a lecturer at St Xavier's, but drank like a fish and smoked like a chimney. Your mother was seven years younger than him. He swept her off her feet quoting that Goan poet, Armando Menezes. They would talk for hours about poetry and music. I told her to stop but your mother wouldn't listen.'

'Stop what?'

'Stop putting out for him. What else?'

'So what if I was putting out? We were all doing it those days. Even the convent girls were at it. Sneaking off to cheap hotels and doing it. It was all those Neil Diamond songs he sang with that breathy voice.'

Cielo and Mummy thump the table, laughing, oblivious of the puzzled look on my face. Their closeness has turned them into odd reflections of each other who do exactly the same thing without even thinking about it, who speak in secret code, and who spring to the other's defence. Suddenly I feel even more alone. I keep my plate on the dining table and go over to the bookcase which has always been here, spilling with vicarious adventures, the self-medication for a lonely childhood. I know each shelf, each worn book tucked in and loosely catalogued depending on whether it was fiction or non-fiction. My parents had nurtured this bookcase with as much love as they would bestow on a sibling, if I had one, and in the nurturing of this fictional world, this world of ideas they harvested, I came to know how easy it was for my parents to escape, if only for a little while.

Cielo has quietened down, and now folding her arms, says, 'He was a *sossegado* Goan man. No ambition whatsoever. My Paulo was the same. Thank God he had the good sense to die early.'

Mummy looks at Cielo disapprovingly.

'What?'

'We don't speak ill of the dead in this house. No matter how useless they were and Paulo was pretty useless.'

Cielo pulls a face, then breaks out laughing.

Turning to me, Mummy says: 'Your father and I, we lived in a one-room flat. There was just this one room with an attached toilet and kitchen space. That's it. In the mornings, he went to work by an over-crowded train. Once, he almost died trying to get on it.'

'I'm sure he was drunk that day,' Cielo said.

Mummy shoots Cielo an annoyed look.

'The evenings we spent on the terrace, drinking beer and having a sing-along. He was happy with that. Tell me, what sort of life is that?'

'What's wrong with it?' I ask.

'Living from one day to the next, without dreams, without hope, marrying into the Anglo-Indian or East Indian community to hold onto to the purity of our Catholic lives. Selling what little property we owned and moving into tiny flats.'

'Best thing your mother did was force him to move here,' Cielo interjects.

'Is that true, Mummy? Did you force him to come to England?'

'Darling, I had to. I was pregnant with you. I wanted a better life for you than the one we had in Bombay. I finally convinced your father to quit his job at Xavier's College when a position came up at a London university teaching Indo-Portuguese studies. Most of our friends had emigrated to Canada by then. I thought he could make something of himself once we arrived here. He never did. An utter failure. Yellow-bellied, good-for-nothing man. Flitted from one job to another, one woman to another.'

Mummy's tongue is the harsh north wind lashing at me. I watch helplessly as she fashions an image of Daddy which I barely recognise. I knew Daddy to be a quiet, contemplative man, who had sought the companionship of books and the tranquillity of trees, happiest when tending to his garden. It was not difficult to see what had attracted my parents to each other. They were the first in their families to go to university, to become self-aware with an intensity which was almost militant, to become financially independent and geographically mobile, and yet they became the limbo generation which remained tethered to tradition and provincial Catholicism. Daddy carried about him a restlessness and Mummy a rebellion, which they, at first, soothed with marriage and then with a child. They often sat reading to each other; later they sat in separate rooms, reading to themselves, tired of trying to reach the other. The rooms in our house grew so far apart, that I felt like I was trespassing if I ventured into territory that was clearly claimed by either of them. The few people they called friends, the Furtados, the Fernandes and the Caldeiras who they occasionally invited over, knew there was something wrong. But they said nothing. Everyone participated willingly in this farce, for who among them had marriages that were any different? Dulled by years of tantrums, flare-ups, and finally resignation, mutual indifference and isolation, Daddy had sought his escape.

I smart now at Mummy's characterisation of Daddy as a good-for-nothing. Daddy is part of me, however distanced from me. It was in this room I'd argued for Daddy when he'd left.

'I wish Daddy was here instead of you,' I'd screamed.

'And what would Daddy do?'

'He'd love me more.'

The half-truth of that statement tunnels its way down through the years to reach me now. Daddy had left. Mummy was still here—for me. I'd idolised his masculinity and his quiet strength. But her shoulders had carried the weight of my listless world all these years. I remembered how small she had seemed after he left, how she had hunkered into a comma at the looming loneliness of being a single parent, but waged a relentless war for the things that mattered: her daughter, her job, her poetry, her freedom to speak her mind. I'd grown up resenting what I thought was her neglect of me to pursue poetry but without her poetry, she would have been less of a woman, less of a mother to me. With poetry, she could access worlds beyond herself and survive the emptiness of her life.

Mummy finishes her rice, places the fork down, and gazes intently at my pregnant belly.

'They all leave, don't they? They fly away after roosting in their own compact little worlds. Their presence in our lives is transitory. But you should tell Sanjay about the baby. Unless he's not the father. Do you even know who the father is?'

Mummy's taunts are in full bloom now, like poinsettias, daring reds with pointy leaves of green, preening proudly from table tops on Christmas Day. I ignore them. Over the years, I've learnt to file them away, and return to them only when my heart is emptied of thoughts of carving knives. Her sneers about my promiscuity are unnecessary and misguided. It's not the numbers which should have concerned her but the undesirability of the men I chose and the rapidity with which they came into my life, their departures just as quick, the damage each one left, deeply wounding. These thoughts swooped down like birds and inhabited me, pressing me to think longingly of Daddy once again, for despite everything, something essential had been ripped from me when he left.

'Did you and Daddy ever really talk?' I ask.

'He didn't have the words for it. He was like a cat whose chords had never learnt language.'

Except I remember now, Daddy's language had always been wordless. It was Mummy who hadn't understood it.

12

Gargoyles at the Gate

That last winter at university, the trees retained their rusting but the cold arrived as always, taking us unawares, dipping to sudden lows and then reviving us with the false hope of a few sunny spells. By then, our lovemaking had turned tender. We took time to linger. We spoke about things that had happened to us, things we wanted to happen to us. I was careful not to insert myself in his dreams. That would be ruinous. I wanted Nathu to see us as a modern love story, cast with an independent woman. The men in modern love stories are anti-heroes. Except, more than anything, I believed Nathu to be my hero. We lulled ourselves into a dream from which we were about to awake.

Nathu described finding Sujata as chancing upon an eerie stillness; her eyes closed peacefully, her cold and clammy body lying inert in a mild haze of cigarette smoke. It was an odd thing to notice, but he saw how much weight she'd put on of late. And that he wouldn't be able to rouse her or carry her down the stairs. In a rising state of panic, Nathu called me instead of 999. I dialled 999 and arrived at the flat seconds before the paramedics banged on the door and carried away Sujata's rag-doll body in what seemed like a blocky white ice-cream van.

Nathu and I drove to the hospital in his father's car.

There was a mini-van ahead of us advertising Dave Fox's Plastering Services. It parked up right in the middle of the road and switched off its engine. A mob of snake-tattooed men got out. Two of the lads came running towards us. They looked fierce. They were going to smash our windows. Nathu was trembling. But we were being silly, we told ourselves. These things don't happen to people like us. They happen to other people; people who dress funny, talk funny and don't assimilate. Just as suicide doesn't touch the lives of people like us. It lives trapped behind lace-curtains and whispered rumours. The bald lad thumped our car with his fists and said, 'Carry on, mate.' We swerved around the van and sped away. Everywhere, London looked desolate: buildings at right angles, gargoyles at the gate, flooded at the sluice, treeless on the heath, and unfolding within the city were tired, lonely lives. Dogwalkers, joggers, drunks, whores—they were all there out on the street, soldiers of the sky, battling the demons of darkness.

'We have to tell her when she comes round. About us,' I said, reaching for his hand; as if Sujata had merely gone to sleep and would wake up to find Nathu and me standing beside her, politely telling her about our betrayal. As if it was the most normal thing in the world to ruin people's lives and entirely within the bounds of human decency to ask for their forgiveness while they're lying on a hospital bed, and expect redemption without them kicking up a fuss. I thought Nathu would say, 'Are you mad? This isn't the right time,' followed by, 'We'll have to wait.' But he said nothing. He withdrew his hand from me and steered the car in the direction of the arrow pointing to the car park. The hospital was all tiles of slate grey and walls of blank white. We located the ward Sujata was admitted to, took our coffee from an unyielding vending machine, found plastic chairs to sit on, and waited for Sujata's mother to arrive. Then, even before the doctor came to us and said she'd pull through, and we crowded into her room and saw the flightless angel lying on a crumpled sheet of white, much smaller than she had seemed hours ago, even as we stood beside her, unprepared and unsure of what to say, I knew Nathu had bid me goodbye.

When everyone else had left, I crept back into Sujata's room. She slept serene on a swamp of sheets under a blanket of blue. I stood sentry alongside the blinking machines, stroking the cannula piped to the IV bag fruiting on a pole. At some point, she flapped open her eyes, clutched my hand and said, 'My father did this to me. My father is responsible.' I didn't understand what she was trying to tell me. I felt only the relief of having escaped unscathed.

13

An Unbearable Distance

Once I saw Nathu coming out of the chocolatier's at Paddington Station, his shoulders squared, his body sparse, his walk spry. Several trains rattled at once from distant platforms, darting in and out of tunnelled darkness, guided by a sense of purpose and destination entirely lacking in human beings.

He melted almost instantly into the swelling crowd but bobbed back into sight a few minutes later, in the company of a well-toned Viking Goddess, sharing the warm familiarity of a long-time lover. He had about him an air of obvious success—a tailored suit, a laptop, a white woman on his arm—as if victory had been easy, and he had fallen, without hesitation, into its rhythmic allure. To hell with capitalism and its corrosive rusting of society, he would have said, the only way to beat them is to join them. Conservative, liberal, neo-liberal, social democrat, what had won in the end? We mustn't pretend we have all the answers, that's what he had always believed.

I followed them out of Paddington Station into the stone-faced realm of regal buildings, hiding behind foreign students who, in summer, appear like sudden squalls all over London. Nathu and she darted into a nearby café on Praed Street, sitting by the window, their unlined faces softened by the lamp-light glow. They looked up from large, laminated menus, laughing all the while, as they placed orders with a young waiter whose sandy brown hair rested atop his head in a man-bun.

I observed this performing pantomime of clichés from an unbearable distance, as one observes lost loves in a fading dream, floating away from the object of one's desire into a cold wakefulness. I taunted myself with all the missed opportunities which were now assigned to other women in his life, more beautiful, more worldly and braver than me. To them belonged the victories of two-door garage houses in catchment areas with the best schools. I counted their wins like fleece-shorn sheep skipping fences and fleeing away from me.

How dull Nathu would find my median-income job at the People's Advice Bureau, arming asylum seekers with information and debt-ridden council tenants with relief. But my job would be a minor failure when held against the larger failing of being alone and lonely. Leaning against the abutting building, shame surged through my slackened body, for what good was my womanhood if it hadn't found companionship with a man? I thought of the feminist icons Mummy spoke of—Steinem and Greer—and felt like I'd entered a time-machine and travelled back in time holding on to dated dreams. Yet, I was a woman, singular, not part of a grand collective, and in my singular needs, I was supreme, I could decide what it meant to be a woman.

After a while, they left the café, their quickening steps like dancers' twirls, suspended almost in mid-air with a weightlessness that comes with happiness. Nathu rifled through his pockets to retrieve what seemed like tickets. She grazed their edges and whisked them away from him, putting them in her bag. It was probably the sort of carefully thought-out gift committed lovers give to each other, not the trashy lingerie, airport gift-shop perfumes and Thornton's chocolate boxes that men buy for stop-gap, mid-afternoon liaisons. Then, without warning, his mouth swallowed hers, his arms pulling her into the warm bay of his pelvis, the safe harbour of his body. I imagined him quoting Tagore to her at night just before she fell asleep.

There broke a freak summer storm which sent Londoners without brollies scurrying under canopies or sheltering in sandwich shops with faces pressed against panes, waiting for it to abate. I saw Nathu and her run for the bus, fading into wet, blurry smudges.

When I got home, I called up Sujata.

'I saw Nathu today,' I said, holding the phone close to my ear, and drawing lines in biscuit crumbs.

'There's something you should probably know.'

'What's that?'

'I've heard a few things here and there.'

'About Nathu?'

'The very same. Attorney-at-law.'

'What is it? Go on, tell me.' I tried to sound only incidentally interested.

'He's been defending some dodgy tax-evaders of late.'

'Oh?'

'Yeah, some thespians who've been sheltering money off-shore. Fancy that. Our Nathu. And to think, he'd rail against benefit fraud.'

A cold shiver ran through me. I could never talk to Sujata about Nathu. I couldn't unknow the things that

I knew about him. Always one to argue the finer points of human morality, he had abandoned even abstract principles of human decency. I couldn't tell her how his courage had failed when he'd found her almost lifeless body, or how he'd cheated on her with me, or how he'd discarded me just as easily. I couldn't tell her that his line of work didn't surprise me at all, that he'd always been able to justify the unjustifiable to himself. I couldn't even tell her that I wasn't much different from Nathu, moving endlessly in anti-clockwise revolutions into chaos.

That night, I dreamt of Nathu, swivelling on a leather armchair. His face was contorted, so that when I looked at him, I could barely recognise him and when he saw me, his expression was pained at my failings. I held his fading face in my hands and said to him, gather first the leaf litter of my dreams crunching underfoot before you judge me. I lay awake in bed, thinking of our time in Hayes. The three of us—Sujata, Nathu and I—harvested from different stock, all nesting under one roof, our lives intertwined by a knot of circumstance, but all headed for divergent destinies. Had Nathu been proven right when he'd said, people are individual, singular, driven by self-interest, and motivated by convenience? What bond did Sujata, Nathu and I carry within us? None, other than that brief time when circumstance drew us all together. Sujata and I were now bound by something pervasive and perverse—the need to preserve each other. Nathu and I had been bound by the intensity of young love which feels at the time impenetrable and yet folds at the first sight of pain.

14

Stale Sheets Salted

It's summer, the days stretch long, the sun tears into our skin. Fruit ripens and rips open on our tongues. The British flag flies from lampposts and balconies celebrating sports victories and royal ceremonies, all flapping in a triumphant collective hurray.

Here in Horton, we are asking the big questions about the future of the nation—about immigration and welfare cuts and foreign aid—but some of us have lost interest and are gazing inwards into our own lives, celebrating our own small triumphs, mourning our own small losses, because caring for long periods of time for things that are larger than us is tiring. In the end, we retreat into ourselves to find quiet. Most of us lead mundane lives; days dawn of momentous significance and yet they dawn utterly ordinary.

The heat is oppressive in the mornings. I lie beached on my bed, stale sheets salted with my sweat, eating chunks of ice which I've bought from the corner-shop. Iqbal, the Pakistani owner said, 'Any time now, yeah?' He placed the ice-cube packet in a bag and handed it to me.

'Yeah,' I said.

'Don't worry *beti*, may Allah be with you.'

'Never mind Allah, I hope the midwife is with me.'

He laughed as he handed me my change. He was

standing beside a 'Horton March Against Racism' poster stuck on the stained wall. 'Be A Fucking Revolutionary,' read the subtitle. Last year, Iqbal had spray-paint graffiti on his shop window which screamed, 'Muslims Out.'

'Will you attend?' I asked, pointing to the poster.

'Who's looking after the shop then, eh?'

'You could close it for a day.'

'I'm not a fucking revolutionary. I'm a shopkeeper.'

'Have you not heard of the "1850 Rebellion of Shopkeepers", Iqbal?'

Iqbal laughed again. It was a tender moment of our vulnerable selves: Iqbal and I needed better angels to carry us to a place of safety.

The contractions arrive like butterflies fluttering in my stomach. I feel almost elated at the ease with which I am preparing myself for an earthquake. I wash myself in scented water and fall asleep.

I wake up to a crimson flow from my body. I call Mummy, who arrives ten minutes later, and seeing the spreading stain, calls the ambulance; medical responders rush through the streets and then hospital hallways, bearing my whale-like body, until we arrive at a labour ward; nurses grow like pillars, needles pipe into my flesh, fingers insert themselves in me to measure dilation. Above me, a din of voices grows; they speak of timed contractions, change of shifts, calling the doctor because something doesn't look right, movies and café menus. Then, a surge of pain—the sluice gate breaks opens, a flood of water wets my thighs, my body splits in two. I feel the weight of a large mass shift from deep within me, snaking its way out. I escape to the ceiling: I exist elsewhere, not here, not in my self, not feeling the waves of searing pain that come without warning, smashing my back against granite rock.

'Take the oxygen,' a nurse tells me, placing a mask over my mouth. 'Your baby needs it.'

The nurse looks at the doctor who's just arrived: 'She's losing oxygen, so is the baby.'

'Take the oxygen,' the other nurses join in chorus.

'She's dilated to 9.'

'She's ready.'

'Push.'

'Push like you're going to poo.'

I watch from the ceiling. I think of Sujata and hope she remembers my directives, because for sure I am not going to survive this ordeal with body and mind intact.

'I can't do this,' I mouth to the doctor. I've abandoned my child already. Why can't the doctor see that I'm not strong enough to go through with this? That I've never been strong enough to be the person I ought to be.

'You can do this,' the doctor says, holding my hand. For his kindness, I bite his finger.

'No biting,' he says, withdrawing his hand. 'Push, when I tell you to push.'

The world blurs with pain. I hear words which although discernible don't make sense: distress, losing oxygen, falling heart-rate, theatre, C-section. Count backwards. Three, two, one. I disappear. A dead January wind blows through me, burying me in the black silt of celestial skies.

It's frightening to wake up not knowing the outcome of decisions taken by unknown doctors; to have huge holes where memory should hold to form a sequence of events. Instead, I have to piece together possible outcomes quickly. The room is lit with sunlight, a bouquet of already wilting sunflowers sits in a vase on a blue-grey bedside table. There is a half-eaten box of chocolates, a tiny pink teddy bear, and a few large-sized greeting cards alongside a floaty balloon which says, 'Congratulations'. By the bedside is an overnight carry case spilling with sanitary towels and tiny clothes which might belong to a doll but are more likely bought to dress a newborn. A pink onesie with little flowers is particularly fetching and surely has a higher purpose than the other plain white cotton onesies. Perhaps this one will be worn on the journey home by a little person. All the signs tell me I am now Mother Earth wearing a smocked nightshirt buttoned at the front. And, I have a daughter. I remember now: waking up in the recovery room to meet her and then falling asleep again.

There are other Mother Earths, sprung like lotuses on lake-surfaces, tending to pale newborns, swaddled like snails, suckling at teats. The air is heavy with the smell of sticky milk and subdued with the hushed tones of visitors trying to restrain their voices, but above it presides a warm, dewy joy absent in other hospital wards. A starchy-uniformed Nurse Jenny enters the ward, and there behind her is a familiar figure.

Sanjay looks about him nervously, not sure where I am, until Nurse Jenny points him in my direction. I squirm in my bed. I'm not certain what Sanjay is doing in the maternity ward but Mummy's suspicious absence tells me she might be responsible.

'Did Mummy tell you?' I ask.

He nods, and whispers, 'We'll talk later.'

His face looks pinched as if digesting large doses of life-changing information all at once is proving to be a strain. I imagine Mummy tracking him down at the Horton Tesco, confronting him in the aisles or maybe waiting till he'd finished his shift, digging her nails into his arm while she impressed upon him with all the force her small body could muster, that his first-born child had arrived in the world. Any resistance from him would have been countered with a lecture about not using protection, about dates and doctors, and the past months having been such a burden on her and the months ahead likely to be even more so. She'd have told him that he better get his useless self to the hospital or she'd report him to the police, knowing as she would that they have no authority over private matters. Mummy was like that; I'd lost track of the teenage boyfriends she'd given a telling-off or threatened in some mild way if they upset her. Now, I was too tired to resent Mummy's intrusions. And for the first time in a long while, I felt utterly alone.

Nurse Jenny clears her throat loudly, and says, 'Baby Souza is in the special care unit being monitored for her breathing.'

'Her name is Ines Souza,' I say with assuredness. Sanjay sits on the one bobbled chair placed too close to my bed, listening intently to what Nurse Jenny has to say, her breath stale with caffeine, her words loud and commanding, as she talks about bowel movement, breast feeding, weight monitoring, hearing test and discharge formalities. She clearly doesn't believe I'm ready for motherhood; she says a health visitor will drop in for a home visit.

Sanjay looks at her thoughtfully and then asks the question I should have asked.

'Why is Ines being monitored?'

'Because she came a little earlier than expected.'

I feel my heart thudding. This landslide of distress is new to me. It's an odd mixture of excruciating fear and a senseless faith in the benevolence of God.

'Is she going to be all right?'

'Yes, don't worry. She's fine. We're just keeping an eye on her. You first-time mothers do my head in.' Nurse Jenny is annoyed. She has other patients to tend to.

'When will she be discharged?'

'On Wednesday, provided mother and baby are both ready. Will mother have support at home?'

'I'm going to take time off to help Anna-Marie,' Sanjay informs Nurse Jenny, as if she were his mother and he the dutiful son doing the right thing. He plays his part perfectly in this parody of disconnected lives connected by an accidental conception. He reaches across the knit-blanket to hold my hand, and smile at me. I withdraw my hand.

'I'd like to see my daughter,' I tell Nurse Jenny.

'I'll take you to her.'

'I don't think I can walk,' I say. My body feels like it's been cut up and stitched back together, held in place by pins which prick every conceivable part of me.

'You should try to walk or that wind's going to build up, and you'll have more things to worry about.'

I look away from Nurse Jenny, embarrassed. Sanjay helps me out of bed and onto my feet. I feel flabby-stomached but weightless, relieved from having performed my duty adequately, but duty to whom, exactly? A new being, who I don't know. I am already afraid of proving myself inadequate. The most mundane of thoughts—fried chicken, shampoos, emails, washing machines, milk, flowers, clean underwear—crowd my mind. I feel foggy, unable to remember things and comprehend simple tasks. When we arrive at the care unit, Nurse Jenny deposits Ines into the web of arms Sanjay is holding out. Sanjay's eyes light up like a streetlamp. He stands beside me, a gurgling brook of delight. He holds Ines' tiny fingers in his; they entwine seamlessly, joined by a primordial bond which speaks through the hollow of ages to all new parents, which grows their heart to ten times its normal size cupping all the love spilling into it.

I smell deeply of her skin, nose through her tuft of hair, kiss her closed bat-eyes. Welcome little one. You belong to me for all eternity. I feel a surge of strength run through me, drawing me into the warm waters of creation, infusing me with a sense of deep knowledge, imperceptible and esoteric. I understand now why Goddess Demeter let the earth turn barren with her tears when Hades abducted her daughter Persephone. For the first time, I belong to a sisterhood of sorts, the fraternity which nourishes, shelters, comforts and advocates for their children through a lifetime of service and sacrifice. The fellowship who recognise each other when struggling with strollers, school runs, sibling rivalries and silly tantrums over ice-creams and juice-boxes. Suddenly, I am part of a vast network of women who strike conversations at airports, on buses, at parks, school gates, hospitals and mummy groups, revealing without hesitation their innermost secrets, discarding their race, religion and political rancour, and running toward each other, deer in a thicket of trees intuiting each other's thoughts. I understand why women worship children above God, above life itself.

Nurse Jenny returns Ines to her cot and leads me back to my bed in the postnatal ward. I clutch her hand and beg her for more painkillers. She extricates herself gently and assures me that a midwife will be along soon to check on my dressing. When her coffee breath recedes, I turn to Sanjay and look into his watery eyes.

He burrows under my blanket to retrieve my hand.

'Why didn't you tell me?' he says, weaving his fingers through mine.

My body still feels robotic, its impulses inhibited, its ability to think dulled by fatigue and medication. I want to sleep for a very long time and not have to worry about how I will cope if the baby needs me tonight. I feel an overwhelming sense of helplessness, and I want to give in to my weakened state, to entrust myself and my child into the care of another human being, at least for now.

After a pause, I say, 'I wanted to. I came over to tell you that night, but you were so cold and distant. And then you broke it off with me. So I became determined to do this on my own. Only, I'm not so sure now. I don't think I can cope on my own. Not like this, all cut up.'

I begin to cry, unable to control the confusing waves of emotion coursing through me, euphoric one minute and despairing the next, full of hope but also filled with dread. Even the thought that Mummy will arrive at some point to take care of me, doesn't ease my feeling of being lost and confused. I need Sanjay, I need him to be part of what I'm going through, I need him to do the things men are supposed to do when a child is born—be strong, be brave, shelter women and children and keep us safe. It isn't right; I don't know the man well enough to embark on such a journey with him, and yet I sense that he feels it too, a reciprocality of attachment, a curious instantaneous bonding between parents which overrides all else. At that moment, unspoken questions and accusations slip away.

'We have a daughter,' he says, holding me close. 'We'll spend the rest of our lives wondering whose nose she's inherited.'

I lean my face into him, and laugh.

'We'll work this out somehow, just give me some time.' He brushes the hair away from my wet face.

Our daughter's birth has excised the inconvenience of our real lives and cocooned us in a caul of oneness. Tomorrow and the days after that, we will unearth the realities that will set upon us like maggots.

15

Forked Lives Folded Midway

The train ride from town feels surprisingly short. The last days of summer put up a brave fight against September but already the evening air feels prickly; commuters scatter and scurry with shoulders clenched. I begin the walk home past the charity shops, florists, hair salons and kebab takeaways lit from within, their liquid lights spilling onto the pavement. The street to my flat is always deserted but the pale yellow houses climbing uphill make it seem cheery even as darkness gathers and a hard fog descends.

Sanjay sees me coming up the street. He stops near the solitary Victorian lamppost, its conical light illuminating his face. His £50k manager's job at Tesco's allows him to rent a decent-sized flat for Ines and me, but it takes its toll on him, working odd hours, sometimes late into the night, ensuring the aisles are ready for the early morning shoppers.

It's his turn to look after the baby this evening so that I can have some time to myself. We've agreed for him to see Ines twice a week. He tells his wife that he's on the late shift on those days. I know how ties that bind work, even how ties that bind loosely are expected to work, sheltering under an umbrella of obligation and gratitude, but how do ties that don't bind work? What am I supposed to demand from a man who is not my partner, or return as favour? What can these forked lives folded midway yield? Whatever feelings I have for Sanjay, I have ushered into a dolorous detachment. I can't become attached to a man who still lives with his wife.

In the lit fog, I see him holding a large fluffy panda in one hand and a six-pack of beer in the other. Trust fathers to arrive with useless things.

'Hard day?'

'The usual. Spuds, spills and soap-box rants from irate shoppers.'

He follows me up the carpeted stairs. I'm aware of his intimately familiar body close at my heels.

Mummy is sitting with Cielo in the living room, blind to Sanjay and I entering.

'What is it with poets and their birds? Coleridge and his albatross, Poe and his raven,' I hear Mummy say.

'You read too much poetry. I have my Bible and that's enough for me.' Cielo's self-confessed aversion to reading comes from a deep disdain for what she calls, 'acting too smart.'

'I saw Poe's raven at my window, yesterday. Black it was with two button eyes.'

'Ravens bring bad luck. Black, no? Black is always bad luck.'

'Ravens bring messages, Cielo. It looked right at me.'

'Are you sure it was a raven? Could have been a black pigeon.'

'I'm not a bird expert. I saw a bird that was black and it scared me.'

'It must have been a black pigeon. Pigeons get mud all over themselves and turn black. You simply worry, no? There's no message being delivered to you. Just bird droppings.'

'You really are a bird-brain, Cielo.'

They laugh.

The flat looks a tip with magazines strewn about, half-drunk mugs of coffee, unwashed feeding bottles and the sour smell of soiled diapers still sitting in the bin. Parked in the far corner is a supermarket trolley with washing detergent, a rice bag and Heinz soup cans.

They turn around when they see us.

'You're late,' Mummy says. Maternal kindness has always been a serrated knife in our family which sooner or later one finds stuck in one's back. She's eager to leave and hands Ines to me. The baby burps loudly in my face, a thin milk-spray landing on my neck.

'I'm sorry, I got held up at the train station,' I lie. In truth, I'd walked leisurely through Horton, and browsed through Shoe Boutique trying on expensive winter boots. The Eastern European salesman had been stiff-lipped and annoyed with my requests for various sizes. But I didn't care. I wasn't in a hurry, or in the mood to placate bored sales-people. I wanted someone to tend to my needs. To slip shoes on to my swollen feet, to press my aching toes—even if by accident—and ask me if the shoes fit perfectly.

The last thing I wanted was to come home to motherhood, which I understood emotionally but not physically: its relentless dependency draining me completely, its practised ritual of changing diapers and feeding, a drudgery, the interrupted sleep patterns an assault on my unrested body, making every bone ache by morning. The only thought that ejects me out of bed, is the possibility that Ines could actually starve if I don't feed her.

'You'll have to try harder, dear,' Cielo snaps, directing her complaint firmly at me. 'Your Mummy here is a nana, not a nanny.'

'Hello, Aunty.' My voice is sharper than I intend it to be.

'I'm only here because your Mummy called me.' Cielo rolls her googly eyes.

'How kind of you.'

'That's what's wrong with this country. You single girls have babies and then you can't take care of them. Whatever happened to marriage and the traditional Goan family?'

'Cielo, will you shut up? My daughter's life is her own business.'

Cielo is taken aback by Mummy's rebuke. She gets up from the sofa and pats down her skirt. Sanjay stands silent spectator to all this, exchanging furtive glances with the two women. He's formed an easy alliance with them which tacitly acknowledges my many incompetencies, perhaps even laughing behind my back and discussing ways to fix me.

'It's hard being a new mother,' Mummy's tone softens, 'but you'll get used to it.'

The woman who left her child alone for evenings on end to go to poetry readings at the local library is now lecturing me on the finer aspects of mothering. Back then, she'd explained it as putting the oxygen mask on herself first before tending to anyone else.

The two women waddle to the door.

'Goodnight, darling.' Mummy waves to Ines.

'We have to get this back to Costcutter's before they close. Cheerio,' Cielo says, holding onto the trolley and shutting the door behind her.

Sanjay takes Ines from me; her little gilled-mouth buries itself in his neck, her fish body latches onto his chest.

'I'll put her to sleep,' he says, easing himself onto the sofa, 'then I'll tidy up.'

The house falls silent. I darken the room to let father and daughter sleep, their bodies layered like tree rings, gently rising and falling in a steady, reassuring rhythm. I take the beer to the kitchen and put it in the fridge next to the baby formula and the Chinese dinner-for-one.

The night is a growl of untethered desire.

16

Spiralled

In the days that follow, Sanjay splits his time between his wife and us—Ines and me. When he's not with us, I think of excuses to call him up. Anything remotely relating to Ines, the flat, anything at all, I call him up. I pray for things to crop up, things which I would previously never have bothered him with, I now ask for his advice. Eventually, I end up calling him without an excuse, just to hear his voice, and he understands this need in me. He saves me from embarrassment and pretends he was about to call me too. We speak of ordinary things and we have ordinary silences, silences which feel like they belong in our sentences. I begin to feel once again that we may have a chance together. I look for signs that Sanjay will end it with his wife and choose me, choose Ines, choose our family. One evening, I ring his mobile, and a woman picks up. This woman I know to be his wife. I can discern music and chatter coming from the room.

'Can I speak to Sanjay?' I say.

'He's busy. We're having a family dinner. Who's calling?' she asks.

I switch off my phone and fall asleep.

The morning is grey with longing, the cries of gulls shredding the sky. A cloud of vaporous fog emerges along the uneven line of shops climbing the street. I sit at Horton's Portuguese café with a cup of bitter coffee and a plate of *pastéis de nata*. The men in the café sit glumly, sagging into woollen coats, as if all the *fados* of Portugal are inscribed on their hearts. I pull out my mobile but decide against calling Sanjay. I pay the bill, and visit his wife at the Horton Library not far from the café. It's small, the library, its thick carpeting making my footfall soundless. I recognise her immediately from the nametag 'Kaya Rampal' pinned to her white blouse. She sits at the far end of the librarians' desk alongside two English women. I place a book by Maria Marcos before her, to check out.

'Have you read Maria Marcos?' I ask.

'No, I haven't,' she says. 'Is she any good?'

'Maria Marcos is a pseudonym. We don't know if it's a he or she writing the books, but it's someone who understands women, particularly women who've been betrayed by men.'

'I see. I must acquaint myself with this Maria Marcos. Maybe it's the man who's betraying women that's writing them. Maybe that's how he knows their lives so well. These women he's ruined.' She scans my book, hands it back to me and smiles. 'It's due back in three weeks.'

After a pause, I say, 'I don't think it can be a man. It's not possible for a man to understand a woman's emotions so profoundly.'

She makes no response to indicate agreement.

'I mean for men to understand why we fuck them.'

She winces at my vulgarity and I too feel ashamed of using such common language but some part of me wants her to acknowledge the primitive nature of women's desire for men, and that its depth and breadth remains concealed even to ourselves.

She isn't at all what I imagined her to be—an awkward first-generation Indian immigrant. She's confident in her job, at ease with colleagues, gracious to readers; her librarian's uniform of a pantsuit is conservative and yet feminine; a few years younger than Sanjay, her luminous eyes, generous mouth and large breasts are that of a sensual lover. I feel like a petulant child standing before her, one that has yet to learn the calm and poise she articulates. In another life, I could see us being friends, talking about books, men, about our dreams and hopes. I wonder if she knows where Sanjay spends his nights when he's not with her, or that he has a child. Surely that is the sort of thing women can intuit even when men hide under cover of subterfuge. Surely this intelligent woman is aware that her husband is a liar and a cheat. The brief encounter reinforces my belief that there is no divine entity who is the arbiter of justice. For there cannot be justice without equality of outcome, and how can there ever be an equal outcome in our case—one that ensures Kaya has a husband, Ines has a father, and I, a lover? How had we all arrived at this place without any thought to the lives we were changing forever?

That night I lie tossing in bed. Unable to sleep, I call Sanjay's mobile. Kaya answers the phone. I don't say anything and neither does she. In this silence there is only shame. I have no way of knowing what Sanjay must feel lying beside his wife while she listens to the quiet at the other end of the phone—anger, impotence? I experience a cruel pleasure coupled with disgust. I want nothing more to do with Sanjay. Yet, I fear what I would reveal to myself when this feeling ebbs away, is that I want him more than ever.

In the morning, the phone rings. I stare at the flooring in the rented flat. It's dirty, there are stains which I've not wiped down.

'Hello, Anna-Marie.'

'Hello,' I reply.

'You shouldn't have done that last night.'

I imagine his stomach swelling and collapsing as I know it does when he is angry. I think of his beauty just then, his eyes, his chin, his chest, and I apologise for my error.

'You can come and collect the things you have here,' I tell him, 'I'll have them boxed up. We can't carry on as we are. We're hurting too many people.'

He's silent for a long while. I wish the words would blow back into my mouth.

Eventually, he says, 'I don't need those things. You can throw them away.'

I think about things then, and the transient nature of their lives, how momentary ownership of them does not imbue them with value; how their value is decided only by our need and willingness to possess them, and how vulnerable they are to abandonment.

Sanjay grows unhindered in my mind; he grows larger, more handsome, more heroic with each passing day. I die hogtied in a sinking bog. I wake up spiralled—spiralling, spiralling, spiralling. I clutch the clothes he's left behind, wanting desperately to inhale of his skin.

When I go back to the library to return the Maria Marcos book, I avoid Kaya, but she catches my eye and motions for me to come over.

'I knew who you were when you came the last time,' she says. 'You're not the first woman to come looking for me, wanting to check me out.'

'I'm sorry,' I say, my gaze turned downward.

'He always breaks it off with these women, so I've tried to endure it,' she continues. 'I believe his lies when he says it will not happen again. But I can't compete with a child. I don't want to deny him fatherhood. We wanted to have children but it didn't happen. I'm relieved, really. As much as my heart is breaking, my suffering is coming to an end whereas yours has just begun.'

She's finished scanning my book. I leave the library shamefaced but also euphoric. Who knows how the heart formulates equations, how it weighs value and worth and comes to conclusions about what loss it can sustain and that which it cannot endure? Sanjay was returning to us: to Ines and me, and that was all that mattered.

17

Unknown Planets Colliding

All winter we wait for knocks on the door. Sometimes they arrive in the morning. Other times late in the evening. It starts with Kiran Mamaji, who appears one snowy day, wearing an oversized woollen coat, carrying a large red box held close to his chest.

He says, 'Hello,' shuffling his feet, waiting politely to be invited in. 'I've come to see the baby.'

I look saucer-eyed at Sanjay.

Sanjay ushers the snow-flecked man into the flat, his wet shoes leave boat-prints on the carpet. He hands the red box to Sanjay and discards his damp coat on the sofa. 'Just a small something for the baby.'

'Mamaji, there was no need to bring anything.'

'No, no, no, who else will we pamper if not the first child from Rampal side. She is our future.'

I clear the toys dotted around an archipelago of playmats. Kiran seems like a kindly soul but his heavy-lidded eyes follow me everywhere as if to take notes about the interloper. All conventionality which says children born out of wedlock should be shunned, has been jettisoned just to get a glimpse of the newborn baby. Sanjay has been forgiven for leaving his carefully chosen wife of ten years and moving in with the mother of his child. Kiran is compelled by the dictates of DNA to seek out his own and bond with it.

Sanjay appears with a floral-kitted Ines and places her on Kiran's bony knees. Kiran floats his fingers in the air and clicks them repeatedly. That startles Ines. She begins to cry and then giggle at the delightful clicking sounds. Here is an elderly man who I've never met clucking over my daughter and wiping her drooling smile with his magician's handkerchief. His swift hands and lean legs safely judder her on his lap.

'So pretty. She looks just like your mother,' he says to Sanjay.

'Yes, Mamaji.'

'You know *beta*, your mother and I looked like twins when we were young, and this little one will grow up to be a beauty just like your mother. God bless her soul.'

I feel briefly excluded but I realise Ines' life extends backwards into centuries-old family histories of which I have no inkling. Somehow she emerged into this world more fully formed than I care to understand, bearing much more than tentacles of arms and legs. She is the catalyst, connected to a whole eco-system of criss-crossing DNAs merging into an accidental amalgam.

'What is her name?'

'Ines,' Sanjay says, apprehensively.

'What sort of name is that?'

'It's a Portuguese name.'

'Are you from Portugal, *beta*?'

'Mamaji, it's a Christian name from Anna-Marie's side.'

'Did you consult the Guru Granth Sahib?'

Sanjay offers only an uncomfortable silence by way of a response.

'It's my mother's name. It's tradition among Catholic

Goans to name children after their grandparents.' I intrude on the conversation.

Mamaji ignores me, his scrawny neck turns away from me and his eyes fix on Sanjay.

'Not to worry, *beta*. We will adopt a Punjabi name for her as well. Your aunty and I will take her to the Gurudwara and find the right name for her, *thik hai*?'

Sanjay nods.

I feel the tilting of unknown planets colliding with my Goan world but strangely the tremors feel non-threatening. Sanjay sits beside Kiran, opens the red box; he uncovers halwa, and trapped under sheafs of soft pink tissue paper is something glinting, a gold bracelet with a *khanda* charm, which Sanjay hooks onto Ines' chubby wrist. Kiran then fishes out a vial of water from his pocket and squeezes a few droplets on Ines' tongue. 'To purify her,' he says, breaking into a broad smile. The water must have been sweetened because Ines smacks her lips.

The following week, a stream of people, more uncles, aunts, first cousins, second cousins, schoolmates, neighbourhood friends, swarm around Ines like protective bees. She becomes in turn Chotu, Sweetie, Gori, Billo, Dinky and all manner of names of endearment. Sanjay and I are swept along on a wave of acceptance. Sonny, Sanjay's childhood friend, his wingman, comes often with small treats for Ines. He can't quite meet my eye and avoids talking to me but he loves Ines. Women arrive in tribes and file into my kitchen to teach me how to make stuffed parathas and paneer. They sing Punjabi songs to soothe Ines' colicky nerves and massage her body with herbal oils. They utter alien words which already make sense to Ines and tell her stories of great gurus and warriors of her race who forever altered the course of history. I am drawn into this village of hunters, gatherers, spiritualists, teachers and nurturers, this intrusion of noisy women and men. I feel part of something ancient, emerging from the depths of time to claim me and my daughter.

There are other young mothers I can visit over the weekend to swap stories. There are babysitters a phone-call away. There are elders with ready advice about coughs and clothing, about rashes and child safety, and in this sterile isolation London imposes on all of us, I start grafting onto something larger than me.

Sanjay stands on the circumference of these conversations mouthing words at me. People can live like that for a long time, talking above the din of voices, believing they make sense to each other.

Sometime in spring the cherry blossom trees near St Catherine's Church turn to plumes of pink. That's when I run into Jassie at Barnardo's charity shop. She is browsing through a rail of second-hand clothes, arching her brows each time something catches her eye. She has with her two small boys who run around the shop playing with a wooden aeroplane they've found in the toy bin. They are very thin and I fear they might break if they fall over. What might one say to a former classmate if they run into them at a charity shop? At Bollywood Style Salon, we can carry on mumbling pleasantries without the slightest interest in each other's lives. We can be civil and yet distant. We can end our time together amicably; she having rendered a service and me having parted with my money. A grubby affair, no doubt, but still an honourable exchange.

Here, in the musty smell of Bernardo's worn clothes and chipped bric-a-brac, it is all too clear that the dreams constructed for us in primary school have collapsed, and that only for the briefest period of our lives, were we ever going to be in the same room as equals. And even then had we ever really been equal? It all comes back to me: Jassie of the dropped-Gs and free school meals, Jassie whose mother couldn't speak English and whose father was always trying his hand at 'business', Jassie who could never afford music lessons or trips to the theatre or summer camp, and had to have the events narrated to her by us, crafted and embellished. Jassie had always had things second-hand, even stories, spat at her, after we'd sucked the joy out of them.

I move slowly away from the Polish woman and her daughter making a spectacle of themselves trying to read loudly from the books on display. I hand the bag of used clothes I'm carrying to the woman with liver spots and the 1950s lacquered hair, sitting at the counter. She looks up at me, and asks, 'Do you want to fill the Gift Aid form?'

'Sod that.'

'Excuse me?' she says, pointing to the 'Will Not Tolerate Abuse of Staff' sign.

'I'm awfully sorry,' I say, 'but I'm in a hurry.' I sound as if I'm at Royal Ascot rather than at a Horton charity shop.

'Still no reason to be rude.'

I smile weakly and head to the exit. Jassie's eyes meet mine just then. She ducks behind a cardboard cut-out of the Queen, ashamed to see me. Perhaps tomorrow or the month after, I will see Jassie in the street wearing the dress I once owned or 'pre-loved' as they call them now, and I will avoid her because it's just too painful to acknowledge failure like this when you're both brown. In that instant, I forgive Jassie for laughing at me. Only something within me tells me that Jassie is still laughing at me. Somewhere in the shadows, I see Sonny lurking about, watching me.

18

Negative Space

Ines and Sanjay are spending the night with Kiran Mamaji. I call Sujata over. She and I spend the evening drinking wine and looking at old photographs. The wine is a cheap red; after three bottles it sinks into my head and sits there, heavy and sullen.

The photographs are of old classmates posed with class teachers and all the confidence of the young. Both of us have proved useless at making friends. There is the question of loyalty. Any friendship will jeopardise us in a way we are not willing to risk.

Sujata talks gaily about some of the students, who although not part of our lives, pop up as Facebook friends assuming a degree of familiarity which we'd not shared in real life, and opening up about themselves in a manner we find vulgar in its revelatory glee.

'There's a face I'd rather forget,' she says, unearthing an already-fading print of Nathu and her, eating at a kebab shop.

'The hummus pit we used to call it.' I laugh nervously at Nathu's sudden appearance.

'He's a right proper git, innit?'

'Is he still defending dodgy tax-evaders, then?'

'Worse. Heard he's advising Tory fiscal policy.'

'More welfare cuts?'

'Maybe he'll suggest we ship off all the poor to a penal colony.'

'What, like a Cayman Island shelter for the homeless?'

We laugh and drink more wine. Sujata lights a cigarette.

'I don't believe it,' I say, 'Nathu the Bengali Conservative, who would have thought it, eh?'

'He was always a Conservative,' she says, inhaling deeply on her stub.

'You knew this about him?'

'Yes, of course, I knew. Didn't you?'

I'd known this too, Nathu had confessed as much to me, but something in me had always hoped it was just youthful rebellion, and that it wouldn't come to fruition, that Nathu would realise his proper place was with us—Sujata and me and people like us, not them. I felt mauled by Nathu's many betrayals of us. He and Sujata had broken up a few months after she'd tried to kill herself. He had proved as callous in healing pain as he had been in inflicting it. Sujata had brushed off the break-up, saying: 'I'm well shot of that git.'

'The wanker. What a waste he turned out to be,' I say, draining the last of the red wine.

Sujata peers at the photograph, examining it from different angles, as if the light would adjust to offer a more flattering picture of a time when we were all together. Life would be so much more bearable if we could just be better judges of human character, I think to myself. Nothing surprises me as much as the undulations of human deceit; once honourable men and women who do dishonourable things and then quite unexpectedly, they can be honourable again, until you wonder which part—the good or the bad—is the larger aspect of them or if both parts are constantly waxing and waning, and the centre is incapable of holding.

After getting her public history degree, Sujata had drifted from an internship to a part-time job curating at the Horton People's History Museum. But when a full-time job had been offered to her, she'd declined, saying the corporate world would swallow her up.

'I love the open spaces at the People's History Museum,' she told me.

'I hope it's not all open space. I mean, there are exhibits there, right?' I'd laughed.

'Yes, but what's important to me is the space between exhibits: the blank wall, the empty bench, the chair in the corner, the window looking onto the street. The quiet turn, the negative space between preoccupations, allows me to think about what I'm seeing and assigning to memory, about what's really important and what's superfluous.'

Sujata has remained loyal to the essence of place, and its ability to profoundly reveal parts of ourselves. People, she feels, are self-absorbed and eager to reveal only themselves to us. All through the evening, we laugh as we had done when we were younger, when giddy hormones had prompted us to laugh rather than wit and humour. She still rents a flat at Hayes, so after we put away the wine bottles and empty strawberry punnets, she calls a taxi to take her home.

'See you la'er, yah,' she says, as she leaves.

Sujata usually texts me when she gets home. But when I don't receive a text that evening, I make nothing of it. I drift into shallow sleep, my head dulled with drink and dark thoughts of Nathu. I am filled with rage about him, trapped on some nether world, circuitous and ambiguous, wintering and withering away. I wake up in a cold sweat and lie in bed thinking of the evening. The scratch of a car on the street is a haunting.

Something had been out of place. Sujata's laugh had been brittle, her eyes shining too brightly and darting without focus. I call her on the mobile. No response. I ring again and it goes to voice mail. I will have to go over.

The night lies exposed in its vulnerability; the Uber cab speeds past trees arcing dark branches, lampposts speckling light, shadows shambling on grim-faced walls, fluted fences ghosting white, supermarkets shuttering down.

I bound up the stairs to her flat. Several knocks on the distressed door elicit no response. The door is ajar but I don't push it open, not straight away. Life tends to freeze at precisely those moments when you're called to action. Later when you recall that time, you wonder why you hadn't been more heroic. You curse yourself for your cowardice and you lie to yourself, saying, there was nothing you could do. After a while, you believe your lie, until it happens again, and your cowardice re-emerges. I stand there for what feels like an eternity, then I enter. The fetid smell of rotting garbage meets me in the hallway. Her clothes lie scattered across the room; the rituals of everyday living have been jettisoned to tend to the disarray of her mind. In the curtained darkness, she is pacing back and forth, back and forth, a heavy-footed stomp, until the very act makes me afraid for her, and yet her body spurred on by some slight, keeps in motion. She cranes her neck and sees me standing in the doorway.

She moans: 'Help me. I'm dying. I can't breathe.'

'You're not dying.'

'I can't breathe.'

'You can't breathe because you think you can't. Do your breathing exercises exactly as Dr Yates taught you.'

'No, you have to believe me. I really can't breathe.'

'Take a deep breath of air. Count to ten. Exhale.'

'Why does everyone think I'm lying? I really can't breathe at all. Help me. Please.'

'Remember this panic will pass. You know that.'

'My heart is beating so fast. I'm having a heart-attack.'

'You're in a room. You are with me. You're safe. I'm going to be here. I am always going to be here for you. I'm going to call Dr Yates now.'

Her face is flushed red and coming undone: the demons within her grow strong; they shrivel small into her vulnerable spaces, they prick her eyes, they creep into her mind and possess her body. They sully the sacred, deface the truth. They are everywhere, telling her she's worthless, that her life is not worth living, that the right thing to do would be to put a bag over her head or break open the spidery blue veins mapping her wrists, that anything would be better than being alive, suffering this dread every day.

My brow breaks into a cold sweat. Being confronted by the disquiet of a human mind is a frightening thing. I see the woman I love, fundamentally and irreparably broken. The shroud of darkness, the sod of dirt covering her lies beyond my flare of light. I want her to mend, to be still, to lie down, to weep because weeping always brings about an eventual, if fleeting, calm. I dial Dr Yates' emergency number and leave a message.

'I don't really understand why Nathu left,' Sujata says after a while, sitting down on the sofa.

Knowledge is not what Sujata seeks. She doesn't care

about Nathu, anymore. But she chooses to focus on him, conjuring up more demons to battle. What she is really seeking is a place of safety, away from the fears consuming her. I shoot her a look which I pray will lodge within her like a hope-filled arrow.

'Because he's an arse, Sujata. That's why he left.'

'You see, I don't really know why everybody in my life leaves.'

'They don't all leave. Your mother is always there for you. She loves you. I'm still here. You have your whole life ahead of you, not behind you.'

'I can't think of a single positive thing happening to me.'

'Then negative space has a place in our life. We can't predict the future. All we know for sure, is that a lot of not-so-nice things are going to happen. But they allow us time to take stock of the things that are good and important.'

'I'm so cold, hold me, I'm sinking into a hole.'

I draw her into my arms. Her eyes spring a leak, her body slumps against me, limp and tired, her head lolls to one side, and in the dark, it seems like it has been chopped off. But the mobile flashes like a lighthouse now and then, and reveals her to be whole. All the quiet of the night descends on us and we sit for a long while waiting for morning to arrive; the past crowding in on us, the future distant and blurry.

19

Stars Sink in Sleep

When Mummy told the story of Grandma Anna's death, it was confusing. She lived a long time or it felt like a long time. She died at eighty. By then she'd erased everyone she knew from her memory. Technically, she died long before she left this world, having forgotten her grandchildren, her children, her home, and her name. She saw priests and prophets hiding in curtains and imagined encounters with people she'd never met. She rearranged the sequence of her life and remembered its triumphs with greater and nobler embellishments until they became fantastical and untrue. She forgot her failures or assigned them to other people so that she remained safe from the pain of having to endure them. She invented injustices done to her and mouthed insults from dawn to dusk, like missiles aimed at moving targets. She became the sum total of a life not lived but imagined, a life which belonged to no one in particular and certainly not to her. Her children secretly prayed for her passing, so that their own memories of her would survive intact. But each day, she managed to destroy large portions of their shared past by spewing vitriol on their present. They hissed like injured cats and scattered to different corners of the world. They committed her to a nursing home where she lived her last years with strangers, creating more imaginary worlds for herself, believing she was on vacation at a hotel, and that someone would come along to collect her. She did not go gently into the night, she went unkempt and unloved.

Mummy said to me, 'I don't want to live like that.'

'Why?' I asked.

'When you lose your memory, that's not living, is it?'

'How do we decide what is worth preserving? I'm sure ripping her from her family, her friends, her home, everything that made her human, didn't help much.' I am indignant that a life could be so easily written off.

'She was a dull woman and she grew to be increasingly tiresome in old age. She'd confront me with the most banal questions—about food, about mending clothes, about marriage—in the midst of my own chaotic life. She had no idea who I was as a person. I resented her deeply.'

'She was your mother.'

'There were patches of lucidity when she wanted to know if I was happy. I saw her as a person then. But you know, the old grow full of entitlement for our love and attention, precisely at a time when no one wants to humour them. I too will grow old and entitled like that and then you won't have the patience for me.'

'You're already entitled, Mummy.'

Mummy clasped my hands in hers then, looked me in the eye and said, 'Promise me this, Anna-Marie, that you will put me out of my misery, if I lose my mind like that.'

And I, knowing Mummy to be the valiant goddess of immortality, promised her just that.

A bugle sounds over the sky. The moons are shorn of light, stars sink in sleep, winds drift in cold drafts, death keeps a night vigil. Draw the curtains, pull the blinds, ring the passing bells, I am abandoned by you who takes the last boat out from this world, your pyrrhic victory over life complete. Let the drummer boy play, let the parish priest compose requiems, let the choir sing hymns, let the altar boys kneel, let the sacristan wait, let the gravel at your graveside shift; my tears wash the tabernacle, my heart is entombed in grief, my pain stipples, my soul convulses, my eyes grow wet in mourning. There in the clearing, I see my father; there is no closing of cracks, no final goodbye, no forgiveness to follow the dead into the half-light of the underworld. You part from him in death as you did in life. Wordlessly. Into his arms I glide, splitting open the surface of my scars, emptying my pain into the basin of his being, just as I did as a child.

Early Sunday morning, just a few days before my twenty-eighth birthday and a year after the birth of Ines, Mummy stepped out to get skimmed milk. The road was a shimmer of green washed with rain the night before, and the car that hit her was a bright red coupé, driving dangerously on a blind bend. A small tribute appeared in the *Horton People* magazine: 'Long-time staff member and popular local poet, Ines Maria Piedade Souza, passed away this month. She will be remembered fondly by the Horton Literary Society for her Saturday night poetry readings at the Horton Library, and by parishioners of St Catherine's Church as the Queen of Floral Arrangements, where for many years she assisted Father Thomas with parish events. A remembrance meet will be held at St Catherine's Church Hall by the London Goan Community Association, on Sunday next, after the 5 p.m. Mass. All are welcome for tea and biscuits. Mrs Cielo Fernandes, her sister, has kindly promised her much-loved mince pasties. Father Thomas requests donations for the leaky roof.'

A car blocks our way on the narrow road to Martha's house. Daddy and the baseball-cap man stare at each other; both full of male conceit, unwilling to give way.

'Let it go,' I say to Daddy.

Ines has sensed the tension and has started to cry in her car-seat. She's not met Daddy before and has turned clingy with apprehension. Daddy is unwilling to lose this pissing contest. Finally, he relents and backs up. The man drives up close, mouthing: 'You're the worst driver I've ever seen. Go home.'

'Home's Horton, mate. Fuck you,' I yell back.

Mummy's burial at the Horton Cemetery has rooted me firmly in London. Homes and histories begin at birth, but also in death. The cemetery is the sobriety of the young; its gravestones tell the tales we are too intoxicated to remember and eager to forget.

In those days following Mummy's death, I'd felt the need to return to Goa, to find there some part of me that was lost, that kept getting lost. Mummy had been the omnipresent shadow in my life for so long, I needed to find her in order to save myself. But looking for her in Goa was a falsehood. I drew neither strength nor instruction from Goa.

Goa survived through Mummy in me, more as a concept than a physical space. It called on me to embrace its rootedness through its music and food and family history, but there was no connection to its geography, its actual reality. It was Horton I was moored to. I knew that now; everything in my life would push forward from Horton, its streets, its canals, its birdsong, its shifting seasons marking time, but most importantly my life experienced through Ines.

Daddy puts the car into neutral and revs the engine, before driving off. He winds down the window on his side and takes a deep breath.

I can faintly smell spirits. So can he.

'It's not what you think,' he says.

'Then why do you smell like a brewery?'

'I cut myself earlier. You're smelling the surgical spirit. Look, I've been sober for twelve years.'

I don't know if I believe him.

When we arrive, Martha is standing by the pale blue fence, older but just as taut-lipped. The years fall away like cliff faces. Beside her stands a tall, twelve-year-old boy, a mélange of white and brown. Daddy says: 'That's Milk-Tea Thomas.' The boy stands scratching his neck, unsure of what to say to me, his sister. I reach out and fold him into my arms, aware that he's uncomfortable with this display of affection.

The house is quiet and dimly lit with naked bulbs hanging from the ceiling. It is still cluttered with mismatched furniture; on a glass-top table are plastic toys of nerve guns, model planes and remote cars. There is a cupboard pushed against the living room wall, its doors tightly shut as if its insides are brimming with secrets.

Thomas sits on his haunches, rolling a toy monster truck down an imaginary track. I can't think of a good reason why I have stayed away for as long as I have from my own blood and bone. He is a precious boy with large cow eyes and a mop of dark hair, and the perfect uncle for one-year-old Ines who has joined him on the floor, picking up a rubber Batman to chew on.

In the kitchen, Martha is stewing meat with carrots and onions.

'Ines and you can have Daniel's old room for the weekend. Thomas will bunk on the sofa bed,' Martha instructs.

'Thank you for doing this.'

'Is Sanjay joining you?'

'He has a managers' training session in Luton this weekend. Next time, perhaps.'

'You are always welcome here, you know.'

I nod, staring out the open window at the well-tended garden. Daddy's patient hands have ordered into submission English roses, peonies and pansies, grandstanding profusions of purple lavender, and tangles of ivy laced through lattice.

I see Daddy holding Ines in his arms with Thomas not far behind, explaining to them gently the finer aspects of English gardens, its colonies of rooks and solitary robins, its bramble bush berries, its holly hedgerows of green. 'Life and death are separated by a thin wafer of light,' he says. 'Light changes everything, you can't see it changing the world but it's there, doing the work it was meant to do. Here in the garden, you can see that clearly.' It is adult conversation, which has no meaning in a child's life, but I suspect he is his own companion now, at sixty-four; the circumference of his life having steadily shrunk without him realising it and become confined to his garden.

Turning to Martha, I ask: 'How's Daniel doing?'

She looks at me with hooded eyes.

'Stocking shelves at the co-op for now. Still struggling to make the rent. He told me he's been in to see you.'

'We chalked out a plan for him. Is he sticking to it?'

Martha shrugs.

'I don't really know what's going on with him. Kids. Soon as they're round the corner, they're off. They don't want to know you. You wait and watch, it will happen to you too,' she says, nodding in the direction of Ines.

I realise she's right. So much of our children's lives lie hidden from us. They live in their own self-contained kingdoms, building their own castles. We fear for their happiness every single day, but really, they're oblivious of our concern. I am discovering that already.

I turn on my heel and leave the kitchen, unwilling to discuss Daniel with Martha, unwilling to hold her gaze, unwilling to enter into any relationship with this woman who I still see as a usurper. I've emptied her of all sentience. Only the slight strain in her voice reminds me that she's human and my father's long-time companion. I have no way of knowing if Daddy has been the love of her life, but we make our lives workable in small ways, not necessarily in exceptional ones.

My attention lies elsewhere, in the garden with my father, daughter and brother. My heart flutters as if perched on a flower, awaiting reconciliation.

That night, I dream of Mummy again. She is dead on the river bank, splayed like a broken branch, brackish water lapping low at her feet. Now Plath, Poe and I gather around her; the wheezing of the wind, the murmur of our prayer begins. Ever so slightly moves the hair on her head. We ask her to awaken from her spiritless self. The hum of our grief grows louder, the chorus of birdsong grows dim. Mummy lies unmoving, her eyes closed, her mouth open. The water ripples in broken circles, ebbing her body away to the river mouth.

20

Conjuror's Trick Gone Awry

'Anna-Marie, why isn't the internet working?' Sanjay's voice rouses me from sleep.

'I don't know.'

'What did you do to it?'

The September air carries the sounds of piteous crying from across the street—a woman, I think. I lie in bed, unmoved. All of human suffering moans the loss of something or other, real or imagined. I resurrect myself from the cold shroud of an autumnal evening, and meet Sanjay in the living room.

'What do you mean?'

'Well, you're always messing around with it.'

'Amani doesn't have hers either.'

'How do you know?'

'She told me yesterday when she came over.'

'That's another thing. I don't want her coming round.'

'Why not? She's our neighbour.'

'She's from the West Indies, yeah?'

'She's British, just like you and me. What are you on about?'

'Look, me, personally, I've got nothing against Black British. I just don't want her around Ines.'

'What's she going to do to Ines?'

'Mamaji won't like us mixing with her.'

'Does Mamaji dictate who we can and cannot see? I don't want to live isolated from our neighbours.'

I am beginning to resent Kiran's intrusion in our lives. Often Sanjay is expected to join him for a Saturday meeting with the Horton Friends of India, a group of three members, or five if Sanjay and I go round to the local pub as well. They've appointed themselves the guardians of Hindu purity. They reminisce about India, Vedic maths, and the rightful place of women, whilst sipping a whiskey soda. 'We need a revival. We've become too weak with our Lutyens liberals in India, *yaar*,' they mutter darkly, and slouch off home determined to organise the next great Horton Friends of India conference. Once, they stood protesting against animal slaughter outside the Bangla Butcher Boys shop. After watching the three old men stand in the cold lashing rain for two hours, the Bangla brothers invited them in, gave them coffee, and tandoori marinated chicken wings to take home. Around Horton, Kiran is known to be a good man; he registers same-sex civil partnerships at the Civic Centre as his job demands, always votes Labour, and volunteers at the Red Cross. His wife encouraged him to form the Friends of India group because he's pretty useless at home, and useless men always find political vigour amongst other useless men. This year, Horton's mayor gave him a letter of commendation for being a model citizen and raising money for charities in India, a tribute to minority assimilation.

Sanjay ignores me; he abandons his laptop and turns his attention to Ines.

'What have we got here?'

'Tea for Mr Teddy, Papa,' she says.

'Oh, let's get Mr Teddy ready for tea, shall we?' Sanjay joins in.

Like Kiran, Sanjay is a good man. He is always doing the right thing. He stayed with his wife when it was just affairs. He left his wife when he discovered his responsibilities as a father. He works hard to provide for his daughter. He takes her to the nursery and for walks in the park. He stays up with her if she's sick. He cleans up after her when she throws up. I should be happy. Except lately, I find Sanjay drifting off to a plane far from me.

Ines wraps her tiny arms around Sanjay's leg and tugs him down. They sit cross-legged on the floor exchanging pink plastic tea-cups and pretending to sip hot, steaming liquid. We are all living in a pretend world. We exist on a continuum of today, patched together by the faithfulness of domesticity. We're flapping birds trapped in an aviary of obligation.

The landline rings shrilly.

'It's for you,' I say.

'How do you know?'

'Because everyone I know is either dead or indifferent.'

Sanjay pats Ines' head. She clamours about him and clumsily clings to his pants, insisting he return to his tea. But he's a giant and she a midget in this act, and he disengages easily to make his way to the phone.

'Yes?'

Silence.

'I'll be there. The Saracen's Head, yeah? You owe me a pint, mate.'

I never ask who calls him. All that I know about him, I know from inference or hearsay. His reticence to share his life is because orphans, he explains, develop a layer of insulation; they can't trust anyone, they have to protect themselves from the world taking away whatever little of them is left.

'It's Sonny,' he says, and disappears to the bathroom. When he returns, his hair is gelled and combed back, and his face free of dark stubble. He's wearing a T-shirt and jeans, and the smell of cologne is overpowering.

'Boys night out, eh?'

'You can come if you want.'

'And listen to Sonny talk about tits and arse. No thanks.'

'Yeah, sorry about that.'

'Sorry is what the English say for everything. If I were dying on the street they'd say, sorry, and step over me.'

'You're in a stroppy mood.'

'Sorry.'

'Suit yourself.'

He shrugs, and heads to the door.

'Why can't Sonny ever look me in the eye?' I ask.

'Maybe you intimidate him.'

'Me?'

'You can come across as snooty.'

'Where's all this coming from? Did Sonny call me snooty?

'No.'

'Did someone else?'

'Just saying. Maybe it's you who's giving off the wrong vibe.'

'What vibe is that?'

'The I-went-to-university vibe.'

'You're sad and horrid. You know that?'

'I don't think you know just how pathetic you are.'

There's a meanness to his tone which frightens me. I realise the derisiveness is a way of filtering me out. Our relationship is not entirely without pattern. This here is a pattern: this unspoken upwelling of resentment bubbling just below the surface. After he leaves, I sit on the sofa, listening to the music pounding from our neighbour's flat. It feels as if boulders are being ripped from mountains and hurled onto my skull; the night edges into an unbidden blackness, until it impels me to action. I leave Ines with Amani and head to the pub.

The night is cold; I pull my coat tightly about me. The length of the road leaps ahead with its Saturday night windows like lit-up boxes, little children playing cameo roles in kitchens and bedrooms, or women and men watching TV in living rooms. The street is a receptacle of hope, its long lanes unfolding and never quite vanishing.

The Saracen's Head appears before me, illuminated like a Disney castle to attract weekenders who usually drive past the pub without noticing it. The air is thick with smoke, the light bright and brittle. Vinegary old men are wound round the bar like leeches; the young and tattooed sit with friends, sipping beers and laughing gaily; a party of hens dressed in feathers and sequins are cackling about their freckled bride's last night of freedom, drinking brightly coloured drinks and twirling plastic penises in the air.

I try to find Sanjay and Sonny but I can't see either, anywhere. I elbow customers out of the way and ask the familiar barmaid, 'Have you seen Sanjay come in this evening?'

She spills some beer from a large glass on the counter, wipes it clean, then nods her head. 'Yah, some time back.'

I wait outside the one loo, thinking Sanjay might come out. But the doorway is crammed with hens re-doing their make-up. Men and women squeeze past the hens and melt into the crowded hallway, back into the din of the bar. On a hunch, I exit from the back door leading to the alley. The night air is singed with the smell of vomit and stale beer, the hedgerow has blooms of leaky condoms and broken glass bottles. The lamplights loom above lovers huddled like fugitives, necking like parakeets, unmindful of passers-by. I still can't find Sanjay anywhere.

I feel guilt clawing at me as the muffled music of the Pet Shop Boys follows me down the road. And I realise suddenly that I arrived here all alone. It's been months since Sanjay and I have gone out together, as a couple or as a family. My lungs filled with cold air, my hands numb, my teeth chattering, I stride down the street, determined to not let things slide any further between Sanjay and me, for we still share a bed and a child. I could make an effort, once in a while, to clear away the toys, to put on lipstick and sexy lingerie and maybe some music, and make things full of promise, like they once were.

I take a wrong turn at Otterfield Lane and find myself on the High Street, where a man is sleeping rough bundled up in tarpaulin. I walk past the man, terrified he might leap at me, but his only concern is the cold as he hugs the concrete grey wall of the People's History Museum inaugurated by Mr Piddy, The Worshipful the Mayor of Horton.

At the Taj Mahal Tandoor, a clot of Goan waiters are shuttering down for the night. They acknowledge my existence in a vague way so as not to intrude on it but merely to touch upon it lightly and unobtrusively. I nod back because like everyone else in Horton, I'm full of pointless politeness. Mr Burrage is closing up his fish and chip shop. He signals to me. 'I've seen him go down Old Mill's Way, dear,' he says, gruffly. I smile and thank him.

I'm feeling particularly jaunty as I walk past St Catherine's Church; a field mouse scurries from the undergrowth and onto the road overlooking the large car park, where great beams of yellow light sweep down on rows of parked cars, lighting them up like a stadium but not as brightly, and in a shadowed space at the far end, is a car I recognise.

I focus my eyes in the half-light and see Sanjay sitting alone, staring into the night. I feel my heart lurch, for it is a moment of utter sadness to watch a grown man sitting aimlessly, heaped like a mound, bracing against the bite of a damp cold, contemplating perhaps the many lost hours of his life.

I turn into the slip road which will take me to the entrance of the car park, my feet squelching in the wet slushy mud, until I squeeze past the boom gate and arrive at hard concrete. I walk past the shiny Ford Fiestas, bump into the rear guard of a Honda; in the distance, I hear a car door open and Sonny call my name, I hear his shoes clapping on the concrete, I hear him running after me, I hear him say, 'Anna-Marie, don't go down there.' But I am too far down the parking aisle, too close to Sanjay to change direction now. A full moon floats up like a big, fat balloon, and all the shadows are gone, swept away like cobwebs; the car park is awash with lurid light, and in the car besides Sanjay, a smaller head comes into view, that of Jassie, naked, luscious and luminous without her clothes on; they see me, their eyes wide with disbelief, and I see the moon crumble away into the sky. The illusion of Sanjay sitting alone returns but the conjuror's trick has gone horribly awry. I cannot unsee what I have seen, and I begin the walk home.

21

This Death is Painless

Sometimes in London you can smell the Thames. However far you are from it, you can smell it, salty in its breath, as if you are smelling its briny marshes but not quite. It arrives like a frayed memory, just there, gone too soon, until you wonder if it had existed at all.

After I saw Sanjay and Jassie together, I have a memory of a car coming straight at me with its headlights on. This memory is fractured, as if the light of that car had refracted and rendered me unable to remember events as they occurred that night. I'm being dishonest here; it's not events that are hard to remember, but that severing of intent and action. That's what fractures memory, because when you look back, you can't accurately sever the connection between intent and action. Even with the scalpel of time, it's difficult to slice through precisely between those two. I remember with clarity how the moon shifted behind a cloud plunging me in darkness, I remember the screech of the car, I remember the grey ribbon of road on which I stood, the thud of the feet running after me, the thickness of the hand that grabbed me and held me back, a sharp intake of breath which occurred on the brink of disaster, but I don't remember whether I intended to step in front of the car or not, whether my foot had merely slipped or my body had frozen. Those things are not clear to me.

I walk home and sit near the radiator absorbing the warmth it dispels through its gills. I don't know how long I sit there looking out the window observing with disinterest wrought-iron stairs mounted on the backend of a building. How strange are the things that come into view when the body is worn with grief. But I fathom within that body a familiar emotion, which I know as rage, and I intuit the tensile strength of that rage, its ability to buoy me, to keep me alive through the night. I sense the tremendous ability my body has to feel unhappiness, and I know this is how my days will unfold from here on, one after the other, in a sameness which reveals to me only the unending nature of unhappiness, and something even more dire, my inability to overcome it. For what would truly unfold if I were to look my unhappiness straight in the eye and confront it? What would I see—nothing but the truth. Then, what would the truth reveal? A course of action for me to take. To tell Sanjay, he can have no part in my life and in Ines' life. Having taken that course of action, where would I arrive? I'd arrive at a place of utter loneliness, of dreary days spent in my own company, going over and over again in my mind, some dreadful aspect of my life, or my many inadequacies and my physical failings. I'd arrive at a place much darker than where I stood right now. Worst of all, I'd become a single parent just as my mother had been. Such bleakness awaits truth-seekers. Who in their right mind would want to seek out the truth? It seems to me that it is not right to introspect on Sanjay's behaviour, nor confront my inaction in any way other than to bear it with resilience. This strength of character, I convince myself is what relationships are about—being able to bear pain, and in time, a different type of strength would grow from this pain, the ability to not feel fear. This death is painless.

Darkness surrounds me as I wait alone in the room. A memory of Sanjay comes to me—that of me in the kitchen. Truthfully, other more powerful images should reside within me, like me lying naked on the bed in those early days, awaiting his arrival, or all the times he'd held Ines in his arms to kiss her, to soothe her, to put her to sleep. But no, it's an image of me in the kitchen, cooking. I am cooking for Sanjay while he is still living with Kaya. I am cooking to compete with Kaya, to prove to him that I can be the perfect partner. I'm cutting up vegetables even though I don't own a proper chopping board. I am sauteing onions and they tear me up, but there it is, a labour of love. Cooking is an imposition on my will, because ordinarily my will would not bend, but love has that capacity to bend wills, and impose on people a different understanding of the self. When Sanjay had arrived that day, he was polite about what I'd cooked, even though I'd made a pig's ear of it all. He ate it anyway, because politeness when you are about to make love is an important quality in civilised relationships. We were being very polite. As soon as he was done with me, he'd grunted and rolled off me, and after a brief silence, he'd fallen asleep. I'd listened to our breathing, calm and even, rising and falling in an absurd orchestration totally unplanned. There was a synchronicity to it, a pleasure with an intense solidity, and I imbued in that pleasure I felt at the time of my listening to our breathing, a meaning, imprecise, something other than the one that stood between us. That he loved me. These, I realise are the sort of imprecise definitions of love women like me cling to.

Sanjay returns home late in the night. It is dark, but a dim street light lances through the window, and with that lank light, like a streak of yellow piss streaming, despite the darkness, I can see the white walls closing in on me. Sanjay is talking to me but I don't understand what he is trying to say. I am confused. I can't see straightaway the problem Jassie and he present me with. I have assumed that his relationship with Jassie will be just another imposition on my will. It's the history of human societies to not realise how bad the oppression is, to think, this is going to be all right, this is not going to affect me at all, so I'm going to go along with it, it's just a minor adjustment to make. If people throughout history have come to terms with their pain, so can I. Sanjay keeps talking about Jassie and how sorry he is about everything. I should ask him what this means for me, for Ines, for us, but I don't, because I don't want to mouth those words. I staple those words to the soft underside of my tongue, until my tongue feels like sandpaper, because why would I want to mouth words like that?

I finally fall asleep when the street lights go off. In the morning, when we wake up, we make love. Reality has a sequence to it, some concrete evidence, and the evidence is that he's just made love to me, and so it must be true, that nothing has changed between us. Afterwards, we speak about mundane things and drink coffee, and it's the ordinariness of life, really, which makes one believe that things are fine, it's this fluctuating between distortion and restoration, the in-between state that one clings to as reality.

The days feel Lenten in the suffering they inflict. I think only of finding Jassie, of tearing her filthy second-hand clothes off her, of slapping her face until it purples with pain. I want to inflict pain on her body, on every aspect of her being which is capable of bearing pain. I am blinded by the purest form of hate and I want nothing short of a tragedy to befall Jassie. Only, I don't have the courage to act on my hate. I try to find out things about her, things I can damage her with. I wish I'd asked about her life when I was still her customer at Bollywood Style Salon, but I'd had no interest in her then. Which of her experiences could I possibly have been part of? Which of them could I understand through the prism of my own life? None. She was the salon lady, and I, her customer. I had no way of knowing our lives would intersect—that one day, that woman and I would share someone in common. I feel defiled, physically soiled, made impure by Sanjay who'd sunk into her depths and then smeared her sap and salt all over me. At times, I find myself smelling of salon wax and hair peroxide and semen. I wash myself over and over again, to get rid of Sanjay and Jassie from my skin.

I hear Sanjay on the phone, saying, 'Don't cry,' and, 'It's going to be all right.' These conversations are disclosures of intent and yet interpretation eludes me, as it does all women who wish for outcomes favourable to them.

I'm too ashamed to discuss this with Sanjay's family. I call up Sujata to see if she knows something from the

Sindhi-Punjabi grapevine. She repeats only the useless information I already have: that Jassie's husband has left her for a white woman. Her brown husband, a bus driver with Transport for London, who only ever wanted to fuck white women but who her parents had forced her into marrying, does not interest me. What good is that information to me? What difference does it make to me if her husband's left her for a white woman or a brown one? Then Sujata adds almost conspiratorially that her husband still shows up at Jassie's council flat demanding to see the kids; sometimes he slaps her around in front of the kids. 'I heard she had a broken rib, once. I heard she's on the prowl for a new husband, because she can't cope on her own with the ex battering her and the boys running wild; one's seven and the other's five. She wants a man about the house,' she says in a low voice, as if to elicit sympathy from me. Speak up, Sujata, I shout at her, my heart has no space for compassion. When Sanjay's not around, I surf the net to find out what I can about Jassie. Of course, there is no information on the net about this woman. She is an irrelevant woman, an insignificant woman. She has achieved nothing of substance, she has acquired nothing of value. I scour Facebook pages—the place where inconsequential people gather to prove to themselves their sorry lives have value—and there I find her smiling face: Jassie with her sons, Jassie by a roller-coaster at a theme park, Jassie at the saloon cutting hair, Jassie at the pub drinking with that blonde, nose-ringed girl, Jassie with her Punjabi parents dressed in a *ghagra*, Jassie outside the Travelodge in Luton, Jassie at the beach in a bathing suit, her breasts pushed out, her legs propped up, her mouth in a goldfish-pout. Everything

Jassie does says, 'Look at me all you men out there, I'm here, waiting to lure you into my honeytrap.' We are not alike, I scream into the empty room. You and I are nothing like each other. We grew up in Horton, we went to the same primary school, but we are not alike. I hold on to this thought that I am better than Jassie: morally, intellectually, in every way that matters. I call Jassie the same names my mother used to call my father's new wife: whore, bitch, slut. I see in Jassie's life, only motives to appropriate mine. I see her filled with bitterness wanting to consume what I have, wanting to devour my happiness, to take the father of my child away from me, to take my flat away from me, so that I end up like her in a council flat with no one to look after my child. But then, slowly, very slowly, as my heart endures the pain, as the nights and days blur to become blocks of time through which I've lived and survived, Jassie moves from the periphery of my eye and into focus. I recall things more clearly: she'd been at the Six Bells the day I met Sanjay. He'd been talking to her at the bar when I came in and then she'd dissolved into the crowd as the evening wore on. The girl with the bad hair, the girl who didn't go to university, the girl I'd thought too insignificant to notice, Jassie had been there all along, skimming my subconscious, a jigsaw puzzle awaiting assemblage. To not be Jassie, shopping for clothes at Barnardo's had seemed such a comfort, but it was Jassie's 'pre-loved' castoffs I had been wearing all these months. Only, I didn't know it.

22

Empty Origami Box

I'll stay, I had promised myself, until my child no longer feels the need to wrap herself around her father. I'll stay no matter what the imposition on my will. Only, I can't stay. My heart is worn.

Sanjay and I try to reason, to rationalise, to compromise.

'Why her? Why Jassie?' I ask him. Why, is the visceral blow that assaults women everywhere. Why her, why am I not enough?

'She's the best sex I've ever had,' he says, matter-of-factly, as if quoting a statistical fact in which I have no stake.

'You're disgusting.'

'She's got a great body. You know Sonny saw her first but he didn't get her. He would follow her around like a puppy. But she only had eyes for me.' He laughs when he says this. He genuinely expects me to join him in discussions about other women. Sanjay can be like that—touchingly naïve and lacking in self-awareness, which makes me feel guilty to expect anything else of him, to want him to feel remorse, or even confine him to monogamy. So much of his sense of self is tied in with conquest that depriving him of it would be to maim him in some way. We fall into cycles of synthetic smiles and sullen silences.

Ines scuttles back and forth between us, parrying the pain with wet honeydew kisses. But children don't live outside the orbit of their parent's pain. They live deep within it. If I don't leave now, Ines will spend her life trying to survive me.

Still, Ines is too young to understand that. She sits on the packed suitcases and wheels them around, their clacking on the floor a depressing reminder of our departure. She packs and unpacks her dolls and teddies because she is incapable of comprehending an ending. Her life is full of beginnings. She holds on to Sanjay's trouser pants, clopping about him like a soft-hoofed horse, sure that he's coming with us.

Wintry mornings can be cruel in London: they dawn a dull grey, slow and slumbering, and reveal the world to be infinitely bleak and emptied of hope. Outside is the chorus of chaffinches and bramblings, and the echoing hoot of an owl refuging on a bare branch somewhere in Daddy's garden. This morning, the urge is only to escape from myself, from Sanjay, from everything that reminds me of us.

Ines stirs slowly against me like a newborn foal struggling with its hind legs. She cries out for Papa. I ignore her and burrow deeper into the duvet. Pain swells and unswells, it thins and thickens, it fades and emerges.

Daddy knocks on the door.

'What is it?'

'Breakfast.'

'Go away.'

'At least let me take Ines and feed her breakfast.'

I relent and ask him to come in. I'm in Daniel's old room, until I can find a place to stay.

Daddy puts a squirming Ines on his shoulders. I watch him disappear through the doorway, Ines' small legs dangling from a height. I hear him say, 'Someone has to take care of you,' and then the sound of smacking kisses and girly giggles.

Later, I come into the kitchen and there's crisp bacon and yolky eggs staring at me from a plate.

'Sit,' Daddy says, and pours me some coffee.

Ines is banging a spoon on a metal plate, her mouth crusted with wheat cereal.

'Martha's doing the school run and Sanjay's sent a Facebook message saying he can take Ines on Friday.'

'You're on Facebook?'

'Everyone's on Facebook.'

'How did he find you?'

'Is it really that difficult? He's put up pictures of Jassie, her two boys, and him, on his Facebook page. She's moved in with him.'

'The flat we were living in?'

'Yes.'

'Instant family,' I mutter.

'Sanjay's a dog. That's what he is.'

'And you're friends with this dog?'

'He is the father of my grandchild. I don't want to make the same mistake again.'

'Well, I'm not letting him have Ines.'

'Why not?'

'I just won't.'

'He'll never stop being her father.'

Like you did, I think to myself, but I don't say anything. Instead I yell: 'I'm the mother who was looking after Ines while he was out fucking Jassie.'

'What did you expect from a man who cheated on his wife and had a child with you?'

'Why Jassie? That filthy, no-class girl.'

'Why not Jassie? Men think with their dicks. You think it matters to him whether she went to university or not?'

'More fool me for thinking a child would make me special.'

'Women think if they sleep with us that will make them special. If they give us babies that will make them special. It never makes them special enough for us to change.'

Ines is banging her spoon, creating an unbearable racket, the sort that for no reason at all makes life seem dire.

'Stop that,' I yell at her, and she understanding at once that I am cross with her, lets out a shriek which becomes an unrelenting wail. She hits her spoon harder and harder against the table, her crying prompting her to choke with a ferocity only children are capable of mustering. The walls collapse and bury me in their rubble. Hot tears roll down my cheeks and onto my trembling lips. Ines stares at me with her teary eyes, she's like an empty origami box; I can feel every crease and cut of her life, but I cannot fill her up, soothe her, take away her pain. Daddy puts his arms around me: 'There, there. You're stronger than this and you deserve better than Sanjay.'

Daddy is right; Sanjay was a distorted mirrored image, a reflection of a shifting truth, with no core to his being, no revelatory pleasures to deepen intimacy, no ability to commit. He was a relationship amnesiac, each day with him began anew with no past and no future. He did not have the ability to profoundly know people's lives from within, and to belong to those lives completely.

Daddy picks up Ines and takes her to the living room, soothing her with an old Neil Diamond song, probably because it is the only one whose words he still remembers. The sun has risen and its rays fall lightly on the windows, making the room seem somehow suited to the lives of children and other vulnerable people, making me feel as if all the aloneness I had felt growing up could be chased away by being in this room with Daddy. I stand in the doorway, watching him waltz with Ines, just as he used to with Mummy and with me, and I see her tears dry up and her eyes become twinkling stars in an otherwise bald face.

After he sits on the sofa, I ask him, 'Why did you leave Mummy?'

'You look at the person…and the person disgusts you.'

My heart begins to thump, sensing a revelation which will hurt me.

'Did Mummy disgust you?'

'Yes.'

'Why?'

'I was always disappointing her.'

'Couldn't you have tried harder to please her?'

'I couldn't do it. Not without destroying myself.'

'Was there nothing you cared for about her?'

'Other than she being your mother, no.'

'Then why did you marry her?'

'You know, we don't expect the people we marry to reveal their true selves.'

'And then they do?'

'Marriage becomes an exercise in interpretation. Spouses are really surprised to find their actions interpreted as cruel.'

'Was Mummy cruel to you?'

'She didn't see it as being cruel. She felt entitled to her expectations of me. I was a simple Goan man from Bombay. I didn't have all the ambition she had for me. So I kept on disappointing her. We're never prepared for the truth about ourselves or others.'

'So, honesty in a relationship is a sham then?'

'Your mother's most honest self was truly ugly. As mine must have been to her.'

I flinch as if Daddy's just slapped me. I look at Daddy's hands which have always been thick and large, the strength they possess poised between brute force and sweet cajole, and at times, the two had seemed indistinguishable. I remember now in Daddy, a hardness which lay under an exterior of quiet contemplation, and which I was so often afraid would spill into violence although it never did. It was the possibility of a looming explosion at home which had left me in a state of constant disquiet. Cruelty can be more than physical scars. It was the emotional pain that I had harvested during my time of living with Mummy and Daddy, which had only festered with the passing of years, that had wounded me.

'I never cheated on your mother though. When we were together, I never had other women. I know she told herself that lie, that I was cheating on her all the time with other women, but it wasn't true. It was just something she wanted to be true,' he said.

A weary lie with which Mummy had comforted

herself and taunted me with, when I'd refused to let go of him. But Mummy had always been self-aware and would have known it was a lie she made up. That's what she'd been hiding from me.

He hands Ines to me, lumpy and warm as a blanket. I kiss her head. He goes to the cupboard in the living room, and opening its doors, rummages around to find two large books, which I make out to be photo albums. He sits down beside me, and all around us the light continues to dapple, making me feel warm and loved. We go through the albums: there's a picture of my grandmother and grandfather standing in the verandah of a bungalow house in Bombay. There are aunts and uncles gathered around a piano, singing. There are cousins getting married in flowing bridal gowns or dark woollen suits; there are christenings in beautiful churches, picnics at hill-stations, dances at club halls and sumptuous spreads at Christmas time. Then, quite abruptly, that life had ended, and what emerged were pictures of Mummy and Daddy in long overcoats at Trafalgar Square, at London Paddington, at St Catherine's Church, stiff and unsmiling. The pages turn to reveal Mummy, Daddy and me as a family, celebrating birthdays and Christmas, cutting cake and carving turkey, but later, Mummy and Daddy fading away and pictures of just me. There are gaps in memory, but all too soon, there's Sujata and me on the last day of primary school, posing with victory signs, knowing our world was already changing.

'You know, no one is capable of judging a life from the outside.'

'I never judged you, Daddy.'

'I know you didn't, sweetie. I know you've felt my

absence in your life, and for that I'm truly sorry. But what I want to say…what I mean to say, is that we only ever know one part of another person's life.'

'You cut me off from your life. You created a whole other life.'

'I just felt exhausted with everything going on.'

'What was going on that was so difficult to deal with?'

'With trying to protect you from everything.'

'Protect me from what?' My voice was rising again.

'From every little thing that was upsetting you—allergies, unkind teachers, disappointing friends, your insecurities. It overwhelmed me.'

'But I needed you.'

'I was terrified of having to parent you. You grew up so self-willed, so unbending, so set on doing whatever you wanted. I couldn't protect you from heartbreak. You wouldn't listen. I saw the look on your face that morning. I guessed Daniel had hurt you.'

'So you abandoned me? You were the grown-up, Daddy. You were supposed to be there, no matter what. That's what you signed up for.'

'I just thought your mother might be better at parenting you than me. I didn't want to complicate your life any more than I had. I feel uncomfortable around people who need me in a way I'm not equipped for. I'm good at taking care of people, looking after their physical needs, not matters of the heart, those I don't understand,' he says, shutting the albums.

'You should have come for me,' I insist, sullenly.

'You were sixteen, on your way to adulthood. I thought it was only right you found your way back to me when you were ready. I'm glad you did.'

He takes Ines from me. She whinnies like a startled horse and wriggles her fat bottom in his arms. 'I'll take this munchkin to the garden,' he says. 'Can't stay cooped up in here all day. There's one other thing.'

'What?'

'Your mother left a letter for me.'

'She did what?'

'Cielo gave it to me at the funeral but I was to wait for the right time.'

'What did Cielo have to say?'

'Called me a useless bugger.'

'Obviously.'

'She said your mother had some sort of premonition of her death.'

'Did Mummy regret letting her bitterness blind her to everything else?'

'Maybe a little. But the letter was more about you.'

'About me? What about me?'

'To reconcile you with a chap called Nathu.'

Kali-Durga Mummy as always knows the innermost part of me.

I watch Daddy walk to the door, hunched and tired, with just seasonal blooms to show as his life's work. I'd always thought of Daddy as a composite part of Mummy. But she had negotiated her marriage from a place of pain and he from a place of anger. And they had never melded for the greater good. Instead, they had existed all along, distinct and separate, and I should have journeyed to their interior in search of a person rather than a parent.

23

Winter Tea Dance

The thing about living is that it's repetitive. There is a day, followed by another day and yet another day. My life threads through these days trying to make sense of it all.

It's December. The streetlamps are strung with wreaths of blinking lights, plastic Santas swing from chimneys, the malls stay open late; everywhere is glitter and glow, silver stars and sparkle, sage and rosemary, cidery drinks and sugary pastries, fruitcake and shortbread, woollen scarves and carved roasts; everywhere life lies suspended between reality and fairy-tale; the breath of ghosts rising in the icy-white cold.

Ines hands me red baubles to place on the pine tree we've bought from the Horton Garden Centre. The tree rests propped in a corner of the studio flat I rent close to where Daddy lives, so that he can babysit Ines while I'm at work.

I tip-toe on a step-ladder and place a white-winged angel on top of the tree. Then, climbing down, I click a switch. All at once, the room is flooded with a twinkling of colour and transformed into a wonderland of light.

'Light. Light. Light,' Ines squeals, banging on a Little Drummer Boy set.

Yet this Christmas is marked by a peculiar silence—the silence of absence. Mummy is not with us and neither is Sanjay. There is a leaden dullness within me, the persistence of which does not lift even in clearest light. Its only purpose in lodging at the centre of my being is to make me revisit the past and attempt to clarify it.

The Christmas Nathu left Hayes for the last time, I had moped about at Mummy's house in a gloomy stupor. I had thought I would mend. As it turned out I had no idea how to mend. No one had produced a manual for the mending of hearts. They were supposed to heal magically with time, like a broken leg. My heart felt more like a severed limb, whose loss of use I would eventually have to get used to, but whose phantom pain continued. Mummy insisted we go to the Winter Tea Dance organised by the London Goan Community Association.

'It's time you met some nice Goan men, good Catholic men of your own kind, in London,' she said, sounding wise and appropriately concerned without really knowing the cause of my melancholy.

The St Mary's Church Hall where the tea dance was being held was old; its once wood-panelled elegance now splintered at the seams. At one end of the hall, a tiny window opened up onto a galley kitchen from where Suzette Gomes was plating *pulau* and small portions of chicken *xacuti*. A long queue made up of sequined dresses and ill-fitting suits hissed and snaked its way to Suzette, clutching their food coupons and chatting fondly with those standing next to them. The line moved slowly and their patience was admirable, as if their entire lives had prepared them for just such slow-moving eventualities. The very essence of their being was one of pleasures redolent with nostalgia. At the bottom of the hall on an elevated stage were four men with black waistcoats and large red sashes, singing cover versions of Jim Reeves' Christmas carols. Under the spectral light of a lone chandelier, elderly couples attempted to bend and twist as the rituals of waltz and cha-cha-cha demanded. Women whose husbands had passed away danced with other women, locked in a stale embrace, seeking the warmth of a human body. Occasionally, someone or other raised their glass of wine and said in a festive cheer, '*Viva* Goa.' And others around them, joined in singing '*Viva re Viva, Viva, Viva*.' This felt like a kind world, but a world distanced from the present, a world which had not reinvented itself but had instead held on to something fading, and the very effort required to hold on to it felt strained and awkward. The young were conspicuously absent here. The young had escaped to universities who remade them in images their parents barely recognised. There were only the old here, struggling with the ghosts of lives left behind on some distant shore, lives from which they had not fully extricated themselves. Each year as they mourned the passing of those who had made the journey with them, a part of their past was buried alongside decomposing bodies in Catholic cemeteries across London.

Being here only made me miss Nathu more. The stifling sense of a community fading away reminded me that I didn't belong here. Only I didn't know where else to go.

As soon as we sat down at one of the tables flanking the dance floor, Bosco Fernandes came to sit with us. I knew him vaguely as someone involved in Goan community affairs, sorting out repatriations of deceased Goans.

'How are you ladies doing?' he asked, his whiskey breath on my face.

The band struck up a Portuguese song. Rings of dancers sprouted on the parquet floor moving in formation.

'Fine, Bosco,' Mummy said, straining to be heard over the music.

'Big plans, Anna-Marie? After university?'

Mummy was only in her thirties when people stopped asking about her. They asked about her husband and how his job was getting on or they asked about her child. It was assumed that her own aspirations were of little consequence. If she had any ambition at all, this was to be transferred to her progeny to bear fruit.

'I haven't decided yet,' I said, shrugging off his hand from my shoulder

'Better decide fast. Our Eddie already has a job lined up in the city that never sleeps.'

'Calcutta?'

Mother shot me an admonishing look.

'No, one of the big financial companies in the Square Mile,' Bosco said. He reached into his pocket and fished out his mobile. He swiped a few times and then shoved the phone under Mummy's nose.

'Here he is. All grown up.'

A photo of Eddie with spiked hair appeared, wearing shorts and a T-Shirt which read, 'Nice Boys Do Fart.'

'Very nice, very promising,' Mummy said.

'What about you, Anna-Marie? Any boyfriends yet?'

I shook my head.

'Well, get yourself a man before all the good ones are taken, eh? Your mother could do with a man in the family.' He was solemn when he said that, appearing to reveal a profound universal truth.

'Patriarchal git. Why didn't you tell him off?' I asked Mummy after he had left to gloat at some other table.

'Because I was brought up to be nice to men even when they are being vile,' she said.

Her mood shifted suddenly. I knew she saw a future cast adrift, abandoned as she was by the very people who had defined the Goan world for centuries—fathers, husbands, sons—the architects of destiny. She had none of that. All that she had endured in the pursuit of liberation, the tearing down of middle-class prudery, the struggle for equality her sisters-in-arms had orchestrated, had not rescued her in the way she had hoped to be rescued. Life, she knew, didn't unfold in one showing but in tiny unpredictable moments of revelation. And that night, Bosco had revealed to her that society saw her as worthless without a man. She had called me needy, but her own world was no less needy. Later, I had heard muffled crying coming from her bedroom. Mummy herself wouldn't have been able to tell me what her sadness was about. It wasn't about anything in particular but rather an unsettling disquiet which floats into women's bellies filling us up at night, until we expel it with tears.

It occurred to me, at that precise moment Daddy would have been with his new family. Daddy had taken decisions about his life and yet remained fundamentally unaffected by those decisions. He had decided to leave, to not be part of our family, and yet his life had gone on, like a river that doesn't break with the bend but flows into other rivers, renewing itself, the perfect confluence which always favours men. Mummy had stood on the river's edge, and watched as all around grew trees brittle and barren, sprayed by the acrid smell of misery. The river had swept past her, carrying severed parts of her, limbs and legs floating on the water, bobbing for a while, until they disappeared out of sight and sunk to the bottom. Mummy couldn't save herself. Not the way Daddy had, not the way, men always do—save themselves.

Winter brings light dustings of snow settling on rooftops and ridges of parked cars. By mid-afternoon, the first stream of sunlight will melt the snow leaving behind tufts of white on grey pavements. The streets are empty, the buses at a standstill. All across town, people gather in homes, warmly wrapped in flannel. Ines and I are alone in our flat. The world turns in circles and having turned forces us to experience it again, as if it has made itself new, made itself wider, made itself deeper to hold our expanding thoughts and desires. Only, it hasn't. It has sprung a leak and any newness has been submerged by the same old tired fears and failings which keep us bound and incarcerated.

24

We Inherit Our Parents

The door to Dr Yates' office is always slightly ajar and I often look past it. Inside is a floating space of light enclosed within white walls, white carpet, white chair at one end of the room and another white chair far across from it. Here in this blankness, Sujata unfolds as if from a storm, sodden and bruised. Dr Yates is a woman in her mid-forties, black-haired and well-dressed. Behind the consulting room is a galley kitchen, and on the landing where I wait for Sujata, wafts the warm smell of tomato sauce, meatballs and pasta. Ines' mirroring eyes peer at me from the stroller.

'Spag bol,' she says.

'Yes, spag bol,' I say, sitting on the stairs with my face held between my hands. Ines looks up at me and I reach out to pat her head. Her hair gets caught in my ring, she yelps and yanks away. In the struggle, I hurt her without meaning to, an act which will be repeated many times over in the coming years; I have no doubt about that.

Across the street, Jassie paces the pavement outside Bollywood Style Salon. She's on the phone, talking, laughing, running her fingers through her hair, naively cheering on her life. Perhaps, she's realised the futility of that cheer. More likely she has not. I don't feel contempt for her, just camaraderie. Sanjay is the vortex Jassie and I are sucked into, sprawled flat and silenced on the grid-panes of his power: our pain is a lie, our rage is a hysteric, our opinion is uninformed. All the while, Jassie and I will believe that the world is a fair and equal place, and that we have as much power as Sanjay, but really, we don't. Sanjay controls the source of all that enables us and so we cede of ourselves to him. The sun gently warms my skin; I sit wondering what it would be like to have that sort of power, unbridled and unearned; entirely an accident of birth. My whole body aches from always having to try just that bit harder to survive, to gain respect, to become visible to people, truly visible.

Sujata emerges from the room after an hour.

'See you next week,' Dr Yates says, half-hidden behind the door.

'Are you all right?' I ask.

'Stop worrying. Honestly, Anna-Marie, you make me feel like I'm a crazy woman with all your worrying.'

'Sorry I don't mean to.'

'Well, you do. You always think there's something wrong with me.'

'That's not true…'

'Yes, it is. You can't even look me in the eye sometimes.'

'I don't want you to suffer, that's all.'

'I am afflicted. I can't ever be okay in the way you want me to be okay. But I'm here. Right? Inside of me, somewhere I'm here. You have to find me, no matter how lost I am—you have to keep searching for the woman who makes you laugh and think and feel, and who's been your friend forever. I exist beyond this illness, I am so much more than this. So stop feeling sorry for me. Just back off.'

It's impossible to talk to Sujata when she's in a fractious mood like this.

'Right, I'll head home then.'

'Wait,' she says, grabbing my hand, 'I didn't mean that. I'm sorry.'

I sense in her the need to rise above the debris of small talk in which I've learnt to bury all our conversations. I've come to mistake numbness for honesty, and I've grown cautious of upsetting it. If Sujata does upset it once in a while, I've learnt to say, 'You're on your periods,' or 'You'll be all right really, you're just tired, that's all.'

Sujata and I walk in the direction of Pete's Juice Bar. Ines' toddler body, drowsy with sleep, feels heavy in the squeaky stroller. The juice bar is filled with young people with backpacks or laptops or books peeking from satchels. I feel old and lived-in.

A young waiter—nametag: Sean—wipes a table clean for us and appears with a high-chair. He effortlessly straps Ines in the chair.

'Thank you, Sean,' I say, 'that's very kind.'

'Tank you, San,' Ines echoes, 'tats velly kinn.'

Ines eyes Sean impatiently, waiting for him to place something or other before her. Sean dips into his apron pocket and retrieves crayons and a sheet of paper. Ines scribbles lines of blue on the paper, delighted with her collage of colour and spit. Sujata and I order juices that come in tall glasses with wedges of fresh fruit in them.

Sujata twists the end of her plastic straw.

'They should get rid of these straws,' she says, smiling at Sean, her teeth yellowed, her skin ashen from what feels like a lifetime of smoking, although she is not yet thirty.

'I'll be letting management know, my lovely,' Sean says, gazing into Sujata's eyes.

How can anyone as beautiful as Sujata be so fragile, I wonder. And yet, Sujata is also the bravest person I know. I'm not expected to slay demons every day—she is.

'You should get his number,' I tell Sujata when Sean merges into pools of waiting lunchtime customers.

'Really? He looks about twenty. Maybe I will.' She winks.

'I love the Irish.'

'Of course, you Goans love the Irish. You both like to drink and dance.'

We laugh, feeling once again the warmth of friendship. Outside the window, the streets of Horton spread like arterial veins into our childhood.

'Do you think of this place as home?' Sujata asks.

'Yes, I do, really. I've not known any better.'

'My grandfather came here,' she says, 'after Idi Amin gave the Uganda Asians ninety days to pack up and leave.'

'It must have been terrifying for them.'

'They had a *dukan* in Uganda, a small shop which sold bits and bobs. Imagine folding your life into a suitcase like that. Whatever little they had on them, some gold and heirlooms, they took away at Entebbe Airport.'

She clasps Ines' tiny hand in hers. 'The whole family, brothers, sisters, aunts, uncles, cousins, landed at Stansted Airport.'

'Did they know anyone in England?'

'No. They'd heard a lot about the country, of course, but they'd not anticipated arriving here as refugees, abandoning their homes and businesses. There was some sort of resettlement camp in Somerset to house them. They sang songs and tried to remain cheerful.'

'I can't imagine what it must have been like, living in a camp.'

'My father had his first panic attack there. He was twelve.'

I sit sphinx-like in my seat. Sunshine blades the tables and chairs. Sujata almost never talks about her father. She feels now the need to explain her demons.

'What did your family do?' I ask.

'They told him to snap out of it. To stop worrying, to man up. I hated my father. Hated him for being so anxious and panicky all the time. He couldn't leave the house in the end.'

'I'm sorry, I didn't know. You never spoke about him.'

'How could I? Do you know how cold the blood runs when your father talks about killing himself? Knives, scissors, anything with a blade, we had to hide it from him. I didn't want to know him. I didn't want to exist on the same planet as him.'

'Did your mother get help for him?'

'We never spoke about these things to other people or even amongst ourselves. We pretended it would all get better somehow. But then it started happening to me.'

'Our last year at university?'

'It goes back way before that. I was born afraid. Even as a child, I was afraid.'

'Of what?'

'You can't explain fear. It's always there. It's a darkness I can't describe.'

'You were afraid of a lot of things when we were young, but then so was I.'

'Except I never stopped being afraid. You became fearless, wanting to take on the world. My worries became more intense and overwhelming as I grew up. Everything was so terrifying, so real and also unreal. I was afraid of life, and how it was bound to disappoint me; how I would disappoint life. I woke up in a cold sweat every night, convinced I was being buried alive in a hole. I scared Nathu. He didn't know how to cope. I don't blame him.'

'I wasn't fearless, you know. I just bludgeoned my fear in other ways.'

'But it's different with me. There is no escaping my fear no matter how hard I try to bludgeon it.'

I put my arms around her, not wanting in any way to take away from the seriousness of her condition. I see an opening to reach across the years and heal the wound which has lain there, tomblike in its patient wait, gaping and sore, untended, unspoken and unresolved.

'I'm sorry about that autumn,' I say, hoarsely. I slump into my chair with guilt; Mummy makes her presence felt just then through Ines who is busy drawing. Mummy had stood firm against the world for me, my sheath of solace, my skin of shelter. Mummy, my protector. Fearful or brave, deserters or warriors, Sujata and I had inherited our parents even when we had inherited nothing else.

'I'm sorry about Nathu,' I say.

'It was a long time ago. I was as unaware of your existence as you were of mine that year. You were preoccupied with Nathu. I was preoccupied with myself.'

'You knew about us?'

'You weren't exactly discreet.'

'Why didn't you say something?'

She shrugs. 'I was lost to myself. I worried only about the rabbit hole I was disappearing into. The more my condition deteriorated, the more afraid I grew. It was, it still is, a foggy nightmare from which I feel I'll never emerge.'

I take a deep breath.

'I should have been there for you. But…'

Ines bites into her crayon with her birdlike mouth. I reach across to put the crayon away.

'Nathu and you had fallen in love.'

'You're not angry?'

'We were all young, finding our way into the world. You should call him.'

'Stop taking the piss,' I nudge her gently.

'No seriously. You should make your peace with him.'

'That's what Mummy felt too.'

She is quiet for a while. Then, she says: 'The thing is when I'm standing on a railway platform and thinking of ending it all, I'm not thinking about death. It's about life that I'm thinking. I've finally realised, the reason I am so afraid to live is because I'm afraid to fail. And what is failure if not a certain kind of death? So really, I'm afraid of death. I want to go on living. I want to give this thing called life a shot. No matter how difficult it is for me.'

'I love you,' I say.

'I know.'

I want to erase our lives—Sujata's and mine—so that we can go back to the beginning and arrive here all over again. I can't do that. But at least, Sujata and I are at that place where life unfurls with the memory of pain ingrained, and we go on living, anyway.

25

Stillness

The road that Nathu lives on is a shoreline of brooding brick and red chimney; its double-glazed windows staring out at new versions of its old self. There's a stillness about the house, the sort of stillness which insulates it from the rest of Britain, and stands as a measure of success in the British imagination. For ordinary people cannot afford stillness. They contend with the bustle of living, and the wages of their sins are noise and pollution and constant change. In stillness is time preserved at some glorious moment in history where life moves neither forward nor back, but attains a purity of thought and pinnacle of achievement from which one never descends. Nathu has achieved this pinnacle of success.

It's ten on a Saturday morning and I'm parked across the road, watching Nathu play in the garden with his son. Any time now, I will be discovered, for this is not the sort of road where an old Honda with its silencer blown out goes unnoticed for long. The boy is about three with all the jubilant cheer of that age, running helter-skelter and tearing up tufts of grass with his bare hands.

'Stop that, Julian,' Nathu gently chides him.

Julian looks at Nathu and grins his intended dissidence.

Sitting in the car, I can feel England coursing through flitting formations of elm trees and dabbling mallards at the duck pond. How gracefully Nathu has become part of it all. He is as far from Hayes as he can possibly be. Away from his kind of people and the choices his people are forced to make. But is there really a kind of people at all? Nathu had always resisted believing that one could belong to someone other than oneself; he believed the Kapoors had every right to morph into the Coopers; that people were always untethering from their past and embarking on an unknown future. Why did I resent Nathu his success? Wasn't the whole purpose of life to succeed? To be able to choose the life one wants to lead. And if his choices had led to affluence then surely I couldn't be cross with him for that? I was lost in the ambiguity life presented, and I had no idea whether I would find answers in people who articulated kindness or those who were harsh but had within them the capacity to reveal truth.

My mobile vibrates.

'Yes, Sanjay?'

'I'm here to pick up Ines, yeah. And you're not home.'

'She's at Daddy's. You're supposed to have her next week.'

'Oh.'

'Don't you have a diary or something where you keep track?'

'Look, it's just that Jassie and I want to take the kids to Legoland, yeah.'

'You could drive up to Daddy's and pick her up from there.'

'Thanks, Anna-Marie. I appreciate that.'

'You're a good Papa.'

'Anna-Marie?'

'Yes?'

'Can I come over tonight?

'No, you can't.'

We laugh into the phone.

Sanjay calls me often these days, telling me how much I mean to him, how much he misses me, how his betrayal is all in my head. I'm aware if he says that enough times, I'll eventually begin to wonder about the shape and size of things, because Sanjay can convince me that neither of these are precise and that futures like forms are indiscernible.

Nathu has spotted me. He walks towards the car, the same person I had loved all those years ago and yet a stranger now. His pace is that of a man in his prime, preoccupied with mortgage, marriage and fatherhood.

He taps on my window. I wind it down and smile vacantly.

'Your email didn't say what time you'd arrive,' he says.

'Sorry about that. I wasn't sure myself.'

'You have to come in.'

Inside the house, the red brick folds away and in its place is a sepulchral elegance. The large reception hall is coldly marbled and minimally furnished.

'Beautiful house,' I say to him.

'Amelia inherited it. Barbados sugar money, I'm afraid.'

At the far end is an ornate period fireplace spluttering flames. Above it are men in powdery wigs peering down in gilded splendour, flanked by leather-bound pasty poets and choleric writers, scaling the vaulted ceiling in mahogany bookcases. A framed original land deed has 1758 scribbled as the genesis from which life sprung forth here, an organism mutating with conversations about plantations, slavery, the riches of the Caribbean, world wars, and then the humiliation of losing the empire. History gathers in watchful testimony, presided over by Nathu and his young family. But this house is still telling the stories of the oppressor, not of those it oppressed.

'So, you get to live in this preservatory of Britain's past?'

'Yes, I thought I'd try a little cultural appropriation myself,' he says, his lips curving into a knowing smile, well aware of my views on the subject. We'd argued at length about it, one afternoon at the bookshop of the Victoria & Albert Museum.

'That's a nonsense made-up concept. There's no such thing. Culture is fluid and should be accessible to everyone. I like my individual freedom, don't you?' Nathu had passionately defended his position, which did not occur to him at all as privilege.

'Appropriation is exploitative and unethical,' I'd argued. 'If you can't appropriate the material production of the rich, then you shouldn't be able to appropriate the cultural production of the voiceless.'

'You don't even know how illiberal your liberalism is, do you? Your moral outrage has become more important to you than the complexity of the human existence, we are borrowing from each other all the time, it's how we progress,' he'd responded and then sulked for a while before we'd shared a large pastry at the coffee shop and made up.

The wry tone of his voice tells me that he has not

changed his views. If anything, his dominance in this house has amplified his belief that he can possess what he wills. But then, Nathu had never felt the need to be affirmed by me or anyone else. Some part of me grudges him that moral freedom. I miss his presence in my life, the dissenting voice which had never led to my winnowing but rather a gathering of the self.

The boy—Julian—has disappeared into the muffled quiet of the carpeted staircase. On the landing a Spanish nanny awaits him. Nathu returns to the reception room with a tray.

'Amelia is away shopping in France. Day trippers, what can one say?'

He hands me tea in a Spode teacup.

'You don't mind Earl Grey, do you?'

'Oh, absolutely hate it, darling. Do you have Darjeeling Orange Blossom in the Twilight Shade, by any chance?'

'I'm sorry…'

He sees me smiling as he sits down.

My hands shake so much, I'm afraid I might spill the tea on the tiled floor, maybe staining it forever. Then, there'd be evidence of my existence in this house and Amelia-day-tripper-in-Paris would certainly not like that.

'I'm not sure what I'm doing here.'

'Seeking closure? That's what you said on your email.'

'Mummy thought it would help me move on.'

'How is your mother? Still the activist?'

'She died.'

'Sorry to hear that. How?'

'An accident.'

'How did she come to know about us?'

'Her neighbour Mr Skinner might have said something. He remembered you quite clearly.'

Nathu serves me a plate of neatly-cut salmon and crème-fraiche sandwiches.

'I don't eat salmon.'

'Should I ask Mathilde to make you something else?'

'No thanks. I wouldn't want to disrupt diplomatic relations with our European allies on account of salmon sandwiches.'

We laugh awkwardly. Then he addresses the black cloud hovering above us.

'How is Sujata?'

'Coping. Each day is a triumph.'

'I feel bad.'

'About what?'

'Everything. Everything that happened.'

'We were young. That's how Sujata sees it. She's forgiven us for our foolishness.'

'That's no excuse. There's no statute of limitation on stupidity. I want to make amends any way I can.'

'What, you mean like reparations?'

'Please don't make light of it. I regret everything that happened.'

I feel the ground shift under me. Regret forces people to exile the past to a dark and distant place. I don't want Nathu to obscure away our past. I want him to validate it. I want him to validate me. I want him to say he still thinks of me in quiet moments, that he wishes his wife was more like me, that he juggles alternative endings to our love story at the back of his mind. But contemplating alternative endings would mean moving backward or forward into another life; every philosophy Nathu has embraced has been about upholding the present and his singular existence in it.

He looks serenely at peace sitting across from me in a fabric upholstered chair. I feel foolish and shift uncomfortably. We have nothing to say to each other, our words lack gravity, flitting aimlessly from one untethered thought to another, never resting on anything of substance. Eventually, we fall back on practised courtesy, asking about people we hardly know and don't care about:

How's so and so…?

Whatever happened to…?

I can't believe it…

Never thought he'd end up as…

We even laugh now and then. The stilted silences, we paper over with questions about our present lives. But we soon lose interest in our present and revert back to people we knew way back then.

'Do you ever think about me?' I ask eventually.

'Yes,' he says, and leans over to bestow a kiss on my head. His lips do not linger as I'd imagined they would, as I'd hoped they would. They feel dry—the lips of a grandfather—papery and perfunctory.

After a while he says, 'You must come over for dinner next time. Amelia is a great cook. French stuff mostly.'

I smile politely.

Nathu has remained connected to me only in memory. In reality, he is unrecognisable. An unknowable chasm has opened up between him and me, filled with the experiences of the years spent away from each other. So many things have happened to both of us, things thrust upon us by life, that to seek the safe space of our youth as a place of knowing or a place of common shelter is foolish.

'Julian and Ines can play together. Julian can be a bit of a terror but we're teaching him to be gentle. He's going to be a big brother this July.'

I say of course, knowing full well that we'll not see each other again.

I think momentarily about Sujata—our lives entwined by skeins of a past but more importantly by a future, however uncertain, fraught and bitter. We are all ever held together by the present and the possibility of a future together, not the predictability of a stagnant past.

Nathu is the great love of my life, the one that lives on in the imagination; indestructible because he has never been called to action, preserved in that one great moment when life had seemed so extraordinarily happy.

26

Poems on the Underground

I sit on the train reading about bats in broad breadfruit trees from 'Poems on the Underground,' and before my bleary eyes swim immigrant names and faces. Old arching spires, hello to you, but you never belonged to me, neither fenlands nor heathlands, neither the hedgehog nor the privet hedge of loamy English gardens, the Norman arc and stained glass of country churches, from Devon to Lake District, I inherit nothing. But to me belong the tubes scuttling into tunnelled darkness, robbed of daylight, rank with sweat, big-bellied with immigrant exhaustion.

Some parts of London carry a whiff of the desert; they are treeless at a stretch; motionless cranes stretch their necks, diggers stab at the earth and dune the land with soil. I'm always relieved when the train nears Horton, away from the bareness of burnished steel and glass. Sujata sits next to me, unusually quiet and contemplative; spears of rain streak the windowpanes, the dank carriage is almost empty as it grinds to a halt. We disembark with Ines half-asleep on my shoulder.

'Didn't I see you at Paddington?' Sujata says to the ticketmaster, who is standing tall at the gate, hands folded behind his back.

'We all look the same, innit?' he replies.

'Not without the uniform, you don't.'

'You cheeky girl.' He laughs.

There's a herd of cycles parked right at the entrance of the station, their handlebars glinting in the sun. We walk past them and onto the road wending downhill, littered with cigarette butts and sandwich wrappers; straggling swathes of grass emerge on either side and eventually succumb to concrete. A toothless man lunges at us from a rain shelter: 'Spare us some change, love,' he says.

Sujata slides a few silver coins into his hand. 'It's all I got, mate.'

'Bless you, love,' he says and limps across the road, with a blanket pulled over his shoulders. He smells foul, of piss and vomit.

'You know he's going straight to buy booze with that, don't you?'

'Then, that's on him.'

We make our way to the canal which is in full spate, thanks to a month of rain, and beyond it, is the familiar field of our childhood memories, which belonged to us before boys and then men made themselves felt in our lives.

I say: 'I met Nathu.'

'And?' Sujata looks at me from the corner of her eye.

'I still haven't forgiven him for deserting you, me—us.'

'Nathu wasn't to blame for what happened between him and me,' she says. 'For most of my life I've lived outside of myself, coping with situations beyond my control. If I manage to occasionally inhabit my own life, I consider that a success. Nathu was trying to inhabit his own life. As we all must, especially you.'

'Nathu became what you and I feared becoming when we were at university.'

'What exactly was that?'

'The establishment. He forgot his roots. He stopped caring about us, about community.'

'You're calling Nathu an Uncle Tom. That's not fair. You're denying him the right to belong to this country. Nathu became what all immigrant parents secretly hope their children turn out to be—a success story. In your mind, he's undeserving of success because he no longer believes in the things you do. Anna-Marie, if we are to grow, we have to reach beyond the narrow confines of our own definition of what it is to belong.'

I've grown accustomed to Sujata being my ally in everything, and I find her reluctance to embrace my version of truth annoying.

'It still feels like a betrayal,' I say, mournfully.

'Why?'

'To lose oneself so completely to the other side. To not want to hold on to anything at the core.'

'And what about you, O saintly one? Not wanting to change, not wanting to examine the composition of your conflicted self, is just being nostalgic for a past conjured up in your mind. In that respect, you're more of a conservative than Nathu.'

'I don't resist change.'

'Of course you do.'

We sit in silence.

After a while, she says, 'We all lay claim to Britain in different ways—unsettled ways.'

She is rocking back and forth as she often does to soothe herself.

'It's okay,' she continues, 'we are allowed to harbour contradiction within us, we're allowed to be schizophrenic. We're a schizophrenic nation under one sovereign sky. Our lives are messy, our loves are messy, our emotions are messy, our politics is messy. Don't worry, the centre will hold, it always does in the end.'

I feel the release of the bitterness I've harboured all these years, the pointless offence I've taken at the choices Nathu had made. Nathu had always seen life for what it was—a construct which was evolving and he had been willing to evolve; our savage past was no more dishonourable than our enlightened present, our former selves no more or less virtuous than our new avatars.

Sujata tucks a stray hair behind my ears. 'Whatever happens, whoever we become, we'll always have each other. With you, I can exhale. The pain within can break free and live outside of me for a while.'

'To eternity and back.' I smile at her and press her hand to my lips.

'I've always thought of you as my mate for life, anyway,' she says.

The clouds shift just then to reveal purpled folds of sky. Ines is tumbling down the uncut grass, pine needles stuck in her hair. There are so many thoughts tangled up in my mind: How do we redeem those we love? How do we redeem ourselves when we fail those we love? Do we still love when all traces of the person we once knew disappear and they become nothing more than a curated collection of old memories? Do we hold on to the sacred parts that we once loved even when everything else is dissolving? Sujata and I had once trusted in the permanence of place over the constancy of people but that had not held true: people, places, everything had changed. It is only through Sujata, who yields to the gentle care of the moment, who gives in to the nothingness of the present, that I've come to know what it is to live. Perhaps, in the end, life is not defined as much by solidity and certainty as by the presence of light. In the distance are faint traces of all the people—flawed, fallen, or fleeting, who've touched my life. Against them, I can see Horton, a hazy patch of land which once had been moor, now scallop of skyline, sprung up from nowhere just like me, bound like blowfly wings to some old memory—a father's cuddle, a mother's bravery, a friend's fidelity, a lover's kiss—that vanishes in the cold light of day into insignificance, barely making a dent on my consciousness, crawling back at night, a moonbeam shadow cradling me softly.

Acknowledgements

My principal thanks to Ravi Singh and Renuka Chatterjee for championing my work. Gratitude to the entire team at Speaking Tiger; forever in debt to my parents, Roque and Helen Cardoso, for their enduring love; my husband and daughter, Savio and Lauren Carvalho, for their love, humour and patience. I'm grateful for the early validation I received when the novella as a work-in-progress was shortlisted for the Mslexia Novella Competition 2018, UK, under the title *The Returned Empties.*